DEADLY HOLD-UP
The Third Art Fraser Bridge Mystery

Jim Priebe

MASTER POINT PRESS • TORONTO, CANADA

Master Point Press
331 Douglas Ave.
Toronto, Ontario, Canada
M5M 1H2   (416)781-0351
info@masterpointpress.com

Websites: www.masterpointpress.com
                 www.masteringbridge.com
                 www.bridgeblogging.com
                 www.ebooksbridge.com

Library and Archives Canada Cataloguing in Publication

Priebe, Jim
        Deadly hold-up : an Art Fraser bridge mystery / Jim Priebe.

ISBN 978-1-897106-60-0

        I. Title.

PS8631.R53D43 2010   C813'.6   C2010-902908-9

We acknowledge the financial support of the Government of Canada through the Book Publishing Industry Development Program (BPIDP) for our publishing activities.

Editor   Suzanne Hocking
Interior format   Sally Sparrow
Cover and interior design   Olena S. Sullivan/New Mediatrix

1 2 3 4 5 6 7   14 13 12 11 10
PRINTED IN CANADA

DEDICATED TO MY WIFE

JOAN

DEADLY HOLD-UP

The Third Art Fraser Bridge Mystery

CHAPTER 1

ON A BITTER FRIDAY AFTERNOON in late November, a strong, icy wind chilled those in its path and harassed them by propelling the lightest forms of plentiful Boston trash in random, unpredictable paths along the streets. Only rugged Bostonians braved these conditions for any length of time. More delicate folks chose indoor activities. Several hundred of them gathered in the Westin and Marriott hotels on Copley Place to challenge one another at duplicate bridge. The bridge players may have been delicate physically; their banter was anything but. Many conversations included phrases like *"Only an idiot would make that bid"* or *"You have to be brain dead to take that line of play."* These words were not meant to be overheard by the perpetrator of the alleged fault. When they were, even more indelicate exchanges surely followed.

Starting shortly after noon on this particular Friday, entries went on sale for the first Life Masters' Pairs event at the Fall National North American Bridge Championships. The business was transacted at four desks just outside the main ballroom on the third floor of the Westin hotel, and the bridge game was due to start at one o'clock.

While entries were sold, money raked in, stories told, bidding understandings reviewed, a figure was busily at work. The figure arrived on the 2nd floor of the Westin Copley Place with a good-sized bag slung over one shoulder. The bag contained two blowguns as well as two darts loaded with immobilization chemicals sufficient to neutralize a medium-sized animal, say a pig or an ostrich. The bag was light enough not to be a burden, old and tattered enough not to attract attention. It was also large enough to hold plenty of cash. A bill of any denomination weighs a gram. Two hundred and fifty twenty-dollar bills—five thousand dollars worth of cash—weigh half a pound. The figure hoped to be carrying, very soon, twenty thousand dollars worth of bills weighing about two pounds. Of course, if there were a large number of fifty-dollar bills in use, the take would weigh less. If folks used a lot of tens and ones, or if the number of players entering was large, the take would weigh more. So a payload of three or four pounds would be no problem when the time came to scurry away.

The figure stopped in a washroom on the second floor of the hotel, made use of a vacant enclosure, opened the bag to remove a shirt identical to those worn by the hotel cleaning staff, slipped off a t-shirt and donned the hotel garment. No one was paying attention, so getting rid of the t-shirt along with a wad of paper toweling was quickly completed. With a heartbeat approaching one hundred and eighty and sounding to its owner like a kettledrum, the figure headed for the employee service elevators, picked up two yellow signs saying "TEMPORARILY OUT OF SERVICE" and took an elevator to the third floor.

The plan called for the placing of the yellow signs at the doors of the women's and men's washrooms, conveniently located side by side near the playing area. If the timing was right, and it had to be, hotel employees would be just finishing their scheduled cleaning of the two washrooms and they would be empty. The added signs would ensure that both washrooms stayed empty for the few minutes that the figure needed.

The good-sized bag also contained two lots of fireworks, each attached to a length of slow-burning Visco fuse rated to burn at five seconds per inch, or a foot a minute. Eight feet of fuse in the ladies' washroom and five feet in the mens' would allow three minutes to light the charge in the ladies' and then get to the men's, install the second charge and light it. The few additional minutes without use of the washroom would be an inconvenience to the players, but they would have to walk a little further for that time. When the job of placing the fireworks and lighting the fuses was completed, the doors would have to be left open to make sure that the noise had maximum impact in the playing area.

A pretty young Mexican girl, also in a hotel uniform and maneuvering a kit of cleaning tools, was just leaving the ladies' washroom. She looked askance at the figure who appeared with official-looking signs. When the figure smiled in a confident, familiar way, the girl shrugged and continued to her next assignment. After completing the ladies', the process was repeated at the men's washroom, right next door. Very little time was needed to accomplish these tasks and so far, everything was going well. The figure suppressed an urge to laugh hysterically.

By now, three of the four desks selling entries had closed, and the fourth was wrapping up its business, serving the last remaining person who had paid for his entry and was waiting for change. The other three sellers had tucked their money and checks away in fabric bags to be carried to a conference room, re-counted, documented, and banked.

At that instant, a clamor erupted, emanating from the women's washroom. The eight hundred players, gathered here to match wits in one of the most prestigious championships in the world, fell silent. Seconds later, a second outburst, this one from the men's washroom, added to the ruckus. A smell of smoke filled the foyer and began to trickle into the ballroom. For a few moments, everyone in the area was stunned, motionless, wondering what had happened. Hearing a noise that they imagined was surely machine-gun fire, many of the players thought first of a terrorist attack, then of the insane killers who showed up periodically in schools and institutions in the USA. Their first urge was to get out of the place, fast.

Within moments of the cessation of the racket, a loud, confident voice could be heard clearly over the public address system, calmly urging everyone to evacuate the premises. Detailed directions followed, and the players filed out in a surprisingly quick, orderly manner.

Two men and two ladies, employees of the American Contract Bridge League, had been selling entries. Three of the group were not quite sure what to do. Hank, the most senior man of the group, experienced and well respected by his colleagues, decided that someone needed to take charge.

"Look. Why don't Frank and I take the money and scuttle up to the fourth floor. We'll take the stairs. The elevators may be disabled. You ladies just go ahead and follow the evacuation orders. We'll regroup after this blows over. There's no point in all of us getting involved or hurt, or both."

Hank's plan was acceptable to everyone. The ladies laid their bags of money on Hank's desk and joined the last of the exiting bridge players. Hank and Frank each picked up two of the fabric bags and were about to leave the area. Unnoticed by them, the slim figure, now wearing a ski mask, approached from behind. The figure took an unusual-looking pipe from the good-sized bag, pointed it first at Hank and then at Frank. Within seconds of one another, they fell to the floor, inert. The figure crouched below the level of the desk where entries had been sold, stripped off the ski mask, gathered up the money bags, put them in the bag, checked to make sure no one remained in the vicinity, and hurried to the employee service elevators. The hotel security guards who appeared on the scene did not notice a slim figure in a hotel employee's garb slipping through the heavy doors marked EMPLOYEES ONLY.

Alan Gilead, well-known genial CEO of the American Contract Bridge League, had been planning to play with his wife, Alice, on the Friday of the first Life Masters' Pairs game at the national tournament. He had picked up an entry early and was chatting with friends when the melee started. Noise resembling shots from an automatic weapon, the smell of smoke, and then a loud order for everyone to evacuate the ballroom combined to create a fair degree of havoc.

Without really knowing what was happening, Alan took his wife's hand and led her into the crowd that was making its way towards the emergency exit. Huddled outside on the sidewalk, they shivered in the Boston cold for eight long minutes.

Players who knew him approached and asked all manner of questions without realizing that he was as uninformed as they were about the events that had just transpired.

"What's happening in there, Alan?"

"Is somebody shooting the place up?"

"Sounds like a terrorist is on the loose."

Alan could only put on his usual genial smile, shrug his shoulders and utter words of hope. Finally, the coast was declared clear and everyone was invited to return inside. When they returned to the ballroom where the game was to have taken place, he saw several directors at the table where entries had been sold. Fred Jardeen, the head director, approached him and told him about the robbery and the stunning of two directors.

Fred was a personable, energetic fellow who had the job of heading up and organizing the whole group of ACBL Directors across North America. Three times a year, when a national championship was scheduled, his priorities focused on that specific event, and he worked on location for all eleven days.

"How are you going to handle the game?" asked Alan.

"The place is a zoo at the moment, but I see no reason why we shouldn't go ahead and run the game. I know we're out about twenty-five thousand dollars, but canceling the game won't bring it back. We've called an ambulance for Hank, but Frank should be fine. It'll take us a while to get the place under control, but unless you have a compelling reason to change my decision, we'll go ahead with our announcements."

"I agree completely," said Alan. "Alice and I had planned to play, but we'd better drop out of the game. I'm going to talk to a few other board members and get them to drop out as well. I need them to join me and work out how we should deal with this."

Fred gathered the directing staff and advised them of his decision, and the players soon heard orders over the public address system directing them to their tables. Absolute chaos was transformed into a state of orderliness in a remarkably short time. Alan saw two paramedics hurry in with a stretcher and roll Hank onto it. After checking his vital signs, they tucked a blanket over him and carried him out. Within a half hour, the ballroom once again had the normal appearance of a bridge tournament: people sitting quietly at the dozens of tables, slapping bidding cards on the table surface and murmuring quietly when hands were finished or when they changed tables.

Fred came up to Alan and said, "Looks like we have matters under control now, apart from our twenty-five thousand dollars. I called the Boston police and they should have someone here anytime."

"That's the best you can do," conceded Alan. "I don't know what our chances are of recovering any of the money. Our insurance may help."

Alan heard a low-pitched buzzing sound coming from the general direction of Fred. He looked quizzically at the other man, knowing that all electronic devices, including cell phones, were banned in playing areas. Fred patted his pocket and motioned him back towards the lobby. "I made an exception today," he whispered as they walked quickly to the hall. "I turned it on when the evacuation order came through."

When they were clear of the ballroom, Fred flipped his phone on, got the number of the caller and returned the call. His face darkened as he listened. When he hung up, he said to Alan, "That was the hospital. Hank was dead when the ambulance arrived. I guess his system just couldn't take it."

"That is unfortunate. Truly unfortunate," said Alan. "We're going to miss Hank. It really complicates matters. And now we have a homicide to deal with. I suppose they will have notified the coroner and the police."

"They say the coroner is there now and he'll look after notifying homicide. We've already let the Boston police know that we've had a robbery," said Fred. "They'll have to tell us what to do next."

A trio of Boston homicide detectives showed up in less than an hour. Bruce Lente introduced himself as a captain in charge of homicide in the district. He presented Julia Baker as the detective who would be in charge of the case and Bill Steele, a senior member of the department.

The three police officers began asking questions and Julia acted as the recording secretary, trying to keep up with the conversation as she took notes. The officers seemed unsure of where to start in their investigation and whom to talk to. When Alan joined the circle and introduced himself as CEO of the bridge league, the trio began to direct their questions to him. From the puzzled expressions developing on their faces, Alan could see that the proceedings of the tournament were totally confusing to them. It became clear quickly that the police officers knew next to nothing about the functioning of a bridge tournament. Lente would ask a question, then, minutes later, Steele would repeat the same question. Julia sighed in frustration as she tore a sheet from her pad, crumpled it up and stuffed it in a pocket. It seemed they would need several days of blundering to get themselves grounded, by which time all of the players would be starting to drift home. When the subject of the ambulance came up, Lente burrowed in and became critical.

"Who was the intelligent person that ordered moving a dead body?" he asked.

Fred answered, "We called an ambulance and they gave him their routine checks. He was certainly alive at the time. Nobody authorized moving a dead body."

Alan could see that they were spinning their wheels and making no progress. He thought of Art Fraser, a recently retired homicide detective, who was setting up a private investigator's practice. He knew that Art had been involved in investigating and solving cases of other bridge players who had been murdered and had top credentials as a detective. *If we can get him, he would be ideal.* Addressing the police officers, he asked, "Supposing I could find a person, an experienced bridge player and a former homicide detective, to act as liaison with you folks? Would that help us?"

Bill Steele responded with enthusiasm. "If he could join our team, that'd be a great idea. That would give us a kick-start. I can see us drifting around for days on our own trying to learn all the background we need. We could still be nowhere at the end of a week."

Lente gave him a frown. "I'm not so sure we want to bring an outsider into this. It may slow us down," he said. "Well, if you are all in favor, don't let me hold you back."

"I'll give it a shot," said Alan. "If he's available, I'd like to hire him and have him join the investigation on a full-time basis."

Steele, who seemed to act as spokesman for the trio of detectives, nodded energetically. Alan left the officers and went off to call Art Fraser.

CHAPTER 2

ART FRASER ROSE EARLY and strode silently to the atrium enclosing his swimming pool. The warmth of the sunlight bursting through gave him a feeling of elation. Daytona Beach was going to be fine, he thought. November in Buffalo was never like this. No more shoveling snow, salting sidewalks to melt ice, and no more car accidents from impossible weather conditions. Best of all, there would be no more bureaucracy in his life. He was now on his own as a private investigator with only himself to answer to, only himself to promote, fire, give raises to, and complain to.

Art's attitude towards his work situation in Buffalo had been spinning downwards for some time. He had begun to resent having no choice in his assignments. He'd hated being told to do this or that on short notice, with no option in the matter. He had talked to Karen more and more about leaving the New York State Police Force and starting his own practice as a private investigator. Finally, when his father died, leaving a property in Daytona Beach, he had promoted the idea that they should move there permanently.

"That'll solve our problem of finding a family home. The place is big enough for four children."

"You'll need another three wives if that's your goal."

"Let's not rule that out. But think of getting out of the Buffalo climate for good. Daytona will be a great base of operations for a private investigator's practice."

"What do you think we'll live on?" asked Karen. "We're doing just fine on two salaries. We're not saving a whole lot. Now my man proposes cutting back from two salaries to zero. I suppose you'll just postpone eating for a few months?"

"Only for a short time. We'll both have some severance pay to bank. I know we haven't been saving a whole lot, but we do have a few bucks in the bank. And I'm going to invest my inheritance so we'll have a regular income. We'll have to watch expenses for the first year or two, but I'll get a practice established in time. We'll be okay."

"I think you're a dreamer, but if that's what you really want, let's get on with it."

"Am I hearing these words from the lady who expressed total frustration with her job as a traffic cop?"

"Traffic management specialist, please. And remember that I was Troop A's leading performer."

"The performer who loved paperwork in all its forms. Accident reports in triplicate. Traffic tickets in quadruplicate. Hair-raising chases after speeding cars. Not to mention an encounter with a knife-wielding drunk."

"I handled him okay."

"You did indeed. Very well, as a matter of fact. But that could have been your last encounter of any kind."

"Don't make it so dramatic. The life of a police officer has risks that other jobs don't. In any case, what makes you think a private investigator is so safe?"

"It isn't so safe. You're right. But think of my offer. I might even invite you to join the firm when your child-raising duties become manageable."

"Can you afford me?"

Thus, they settled the issue of the move to Daytona Beach.

Karen was now in her middle thirties. As her pregnancy had progressed, she had tried to think of a good scheme where she could engage in part-time work during her child's preschool years. She firmly believed that a mother belonged with her children until they were off to school. The New York State Police had policies covering leave of absence for expectant mothers, but were not offering part-time assignments for new mothers. Karen quickly realized that the arrangement to resign her position with the New York State Police and to move to Florida with Art fit her desires perfectly.

When Clive came along, she loved having time with him. He was a joy to be with. She loved his burps and smiles, more so because they were mostly indistinguishable. She felt flattered when Art took on a gentle attitude in the latter part of her pregnancy, and tried to do everything possible to make her comfortable. He seemed to have completely forgotten his role as a macho homicide detective who was about to become a tough private investigator.

When Art announced his decision to retire from the New York State Police Force, his boss in Buffalo, Gordon Bryder, had shaken his head, pronounced him naïve, and told him, "You've been reading too many mystery books, my friend. How much do you think a private investigator earns?"

"Enough," had replied Art. He knew that Bryder cared little about the earnings of his men. The important thing was to employ people on staff who made the chief look good. Otherwise, Bryder would unload a man at a moment's notice. Firing was now nearly impossible as a result of police unions and other restrictions, but Bryder had half a dozen ways of rerouting unwanted staff. There were menial jobs, remote locations, undesirable shifts, hated pairings, and a number of other ways to reward someone who did not meet Bryder's standards of performance. Bryder was tough, and few officers would admit that they liked working in his department, but no one denied that he was a good cop.

"The median runs thirty to thirty-five thousand. Unless you're a computer guru. Then a top-notch man might earn sixty. You pay your own benefits and travel expenses. Pension, medical expenses, dental plans, you get to look after all of those yourself. If I had known that that was the kind of deal you wanted, I could have set it up and gotten a lot of brownie points from Albany."

"Nobody becomes a detective to get rich," Art had responded. "In any case, I wasn't planning to aim for the median. What does a median mean anyway? The median for police officers all over the US is about the same as for private investigators. Take a look at the top half of the private investigator group. What would you guess their earnings amount to? Double or triple that of the whole group average? I might shoot for that. I don't expect instant success, but we should be okay." Fraser declined to mention that his father had recently died and left him sole heir to an estate of just over a million dollars, plus the handsome property in Daytona Beach. The elder Fraser, like so many depression survivors, spent very little and saved every cent he could from his salary as a university professor. Art reckoned that he, his wife Karen, and his new son Clive could live just fine while he was building up a business.

Bryder had risen from his chair and walked around his desk to shake hands with Fraser. "You always have a point. Let me wish you the best of luck. You're a smart guy and a hell of a good cop." That was the biggest praise Art had drawn from Bryder in all the years they had worked together.

An hour after he entered the residence in Daytona and started organizing his new home, he heard a knock on the door. A van from a local nursery was in the laneway, and a young lad stood on the porch with a small lemon tree in each hand.

"Mr. Fraser?" he asked.

"That's me," admitted Art.

"Couple of trees for you. Can you sign for me?"

Art did as he was asked. He removed a card from a branch and looked at the curt wording.

> *Art*
> *We're holding your job open during your one-year sabbatical.*
> *Bryder*

The deliveryman added, "Take a look. These are very good quality. Seven gallon plants. Very healthy. You'll have lemons next year. Won't make you rich, but you'll have lemons."

Art looked closely at the robust plants. He was not an avid gardener, but he could appreciate the quality of the specimens. The idea that Bryder would take time out for this kind of personal touch moved him. He decided to plant them before doing anything else.

Furniture from Buffalo had shown up two days after they arrived in Daytona Beach. Art and Karen were proud owners of two sets of furniture for most of the rooms in their newly acquired house. Art's parents had filled the house with austere, good quality pieces. He and Karen had made a few of the difficult decisions on what to keep, and what they would replace from their Buffalo belongings, and they decided he should start the sorting process in the kitchen.

He unpacked boxes from the Buffalo shipment and moved discarded items to the garage, organized the pieces that were staying, and then took a break. Karen and Clive were still sleeping. Clive was only four weeks old, and Karen was not at full strength yet. Art made a mental note to remind Karen of the booby traps around the pool area, including the hard ceramic floor and six feet of water. Fire ants on the lawn were something else they never had seen in Buffalo. He and Karen were going to have to be extra careful with a bunch of things to ensure that there would be no accidents involving Clive.

Art sipped liquid he had prepared in his newly acquired Espresso machine. No coffee guru would give him high grades for his brew, but he had his own personal ideas about the roast (dark Colombian), the strength (robust but not biting) and the quantity he wanted to drink (large). He felt that he had purchased a good machine, and the beverage it produced far surpassed the insipid brown fluids that one normally encountered. Besides, it complemented seven-grain toast, which, lathered with peanut butter and seedless raspberry jelly, made his favorite breakfast. He rubbed a tender spot on his back as he mentally prepared to deal with the remaining boxes of furniture, clothing, and household goods stacked in the living room. By his calculations, he should have the whole house set up in three or four days. It would be hard physical work, but he felt up to it.

When Karen rose to fuss and look after Clive, Fraser prepared a breakfast of eggs and toast for her, and then resumed his task of unpacking cartons from their Buffalo apartment. Next on his list was living-room furniture. Repeating the process he had completed in the kitchen, Art managed to set up the living room the way that he and Karen had decided, got the excess furniture out to the garage along with packing boxes, and adjourned for lunch. Once again, he served as cook and waiter to prepare simple things that he knew Karen would like. Art had washed the dishes after lunch and was putting finishing touches on tidying the kitchen when the phone rang. Karen picked it up, exchanged pleasantries and handed the phone to Art, saying, "It's Alan Gilead for you."

Art had met Alan Gilead, CEO of the American Contract Bridge League, on several occasions, and they had established a friendly relationship. Alan had known about the recent murders of ACBL members and knew all of the details concerning Art's involvement in solving the cases. He had phoned Art to congratulate him when the cases were solved and had always announced himself as a fan of Art's work.

"Hi—"

"Art, we need you here right away."

"Where's here?"

"I'm in Boston at the Westin. We have a very rough situation here. We're just starting the Fall Nationals. The Life Masters Pairs is on today. Someone robbed us right at the start of the game. We took in over twenty thousand bucks. A guy with a ski mask on comes in and disables the two directors in charge of the cash and walks off with everything."

"What do you mean, disabled?"

"He used animal immobilization darts. You know, the kind veterinarians use. I'll tell you everything when you get here."

"You're assuming that I'll get there. How could he get away with a big crowd around?" asked Art.

"You'd think he couldn't, but he distracted everyone."

"How did he manage that?"

"First of all, there was a fire in the ladies' washroom off the ballroom where we held the game. Smoke comes pouring out of the room and a couple of directors rush over to see what's happening. Then a bunch of fireworks go off in the men's washroom and more directors go over to check. The fireworks started a good-sized fire there as well. This all happened minutes before game time. It seems like someone set off a whole carload of firecrackers—the giant size—in each washroom. It sounded like a couple of automatic weapons were being fired. The fire alarm went off and the hotel management decided that the place had to be evacuated. Everyone on the convention floor was ordered out onto the street. Nobody knew what was going on. People got scared and started to take off. As far as we can tell, the guy masterminding this got the money, all of it, and disappeared in the crowd. He was wearing a ski mask, and somehow he got it off without anyone having a look at him. Nobody has been able to identify him. Not even close. Hank Mackeen and Frank Langill were selling entries. They were left all alone with the money. They were slow to leave because they were gathering up all of the cash and checks—unlucky for them. Both were shot with darts. They were unconscious for almost an hour. When they came to, they were groggy and could hardly remember anything. Finally they regained their senses. All they could remember was catching a glimpse of a thin guy with a ski mask."

"So Frank and Hank are okay?"

"That's what I'm coming to, Art. The hospital reported that Hank was dead on arrival. We were having him sent to a hospital and I guess his system couldn't take the shock. This is a terrible blow. But hear me out. When the Boston police found they had to deal with a homicide, they sent a trio of detectives over. We filled them in on what happened. They're like a flock of lost sheep. They know nothing about bridge tournaments, the ACBL, or how bridge players behave. They agreed completely that they could work much better if we had a point man available full time to work with them. Your name came to my mind right away. Bridge background and top homicide man. Put your unpacking on hold. Tell me what you need to get up here and help us."

"Not so fast. You say Frank is fine and Hank died?"

"We found them both lying on the floor under the table where they were selling entries. We thought they were both dead at first, and we got a doctor over right away. He checked their vital signs, and both seemed okay. They were groggy for a while but when they came to, there seemed to be no lasting effects. We were still concerned about Hank. He had chronic asthma and was not all that robust physically, so we got him into an ambulance. Frank's health is good and he keeps himself in pretty good condition."

"Nobody else saw or heard anything? Nobody came forward as a witness? And your robber got clean away?"

"He got clean away. The gun was quiet, or at least nobody heard a report from it with all the fireworks making noise and commotion. Don't forget the hotel PA system was blaring out repeated instructions to evacuate the place. The area was just a mess of confusion. Nobody was aware of what happened. The other directors got back after the evacuation was called off and saw Hank and Frank on the floor. It took a while to piece all the facts together. Then one of the guys called the police."

"I'm glad that Frank, at least, is okay. And what is it you want from me?"

"You've set up your own business now as a private investigator, right?"

"I'm about to."

"We want your expertise to help sort this out. I'm going into an emergency board meeting right away. I'd like to report that we've engaged you to work with the Boston homicide group. We need to get an investigation underway pronto. There are a ton of items for you to handle. We want you up here."

"Hell, we're just moving in. I'm still unpacking our belongings. Karen can't do that heavy work. Clive is a month old and she's got to look after him."

"I got you at a bad time."

"It's a good time for us. I don't need any complications right now."

"I know what you mean. We've all been there. Take another look, Art. How bad can it be? Suppose you put off your project there for a week or so. Finish when you get back. I've already spoken to a couple of board members and they agree that you're the best choice for someone to help us. I'm going to meet with the rest of the board and give them the same message. They'll support me. They have to. This is a crisis. We can work out the financial details. I'm pretty sure that you'll be happy with them."

"You think we can solve this thing in one week?"

"If we don't, we'll never solve it. We have to get going while all the players are still here. Once folks go home, we'll have real trouble nailing down the culprits."

"Listen, Alan. You know how I feel about the ACBL. Nothing but good vibes. I'd help out under any reasonable conditions. But just stop and think about this. Clive is four weeks old. Karen is not at full strength yet. She needs me here until she gets back to normal. I couldn't possibly desert her right now."

"I understand what you're saying. But how about bringing your family along? We'll give you a big suite with room enough for you all. We'll put everyone up for the duration. Art, we have no one else with your background to call on."

"I don't even have a license to practice yet. We just moved down here."

"What would a license do for you? You don't need a license to accept a contract with us. Think it over."

"Call me back in half an hour. I'll have to discuss this with Karen."

"Fine." Alan resigned himself to Art's firm position and hung up.

"Did you catch any of that?" asked Art.

Karen replied, "I caught your part. Alan wants you. You don't want him."

"They've had a robbery and a killing at the Nationals in Boston. He wants me to come up there and help out. Someone set up a phony emergency with a paper fire and firecrackers and shot Hank Mackeen and Frank Langill with some kind of animal immobilization gun. When they were unconscious and the rest of the room was in a panic, he made off with over twenty thousand bucks of ACBL money. The worst part of Alan's story is that Hank's system couldn't stand the shock of the immobilization drugs. He's dead."

"Why don't you go? I can hold the fort here. You've been sweet to make meals and clean up. You can unpack most of the stuff tonight and move the rest to the garage. Just do what you can. We can leave everything else where it is until this blows over. I really feel strong enough to look after things. Clive is so tiny he won't be a problem at all. You'll never get your business off the ground if you develop a habit of turning away customers."

"I'd rather do local work."

"Fussy, fussy. When Alan calls back, why you don't just tell him you'll be there tomorrow."

"He said he would put all three of us up in the presidential suite. They usually use that facility for hospitality during the tournament. He says they'll cancel the partying and turn the suite over to us."

"Let me think that over. The main event is for you to get yourself to Boston and dig into the problems there."

When Gilead called back, Art told him, "Karen agrees that I should come. She wants to stay here, at least for now. I'll get right on the job of getting a flight. I hope I can get one on such short notice. I'll fill you in on my flight arrangements by e-mail when I get them. I'll see you tomorrow if all goes well."

"Need any help with travel arrangements?"

"We can do that part."

"Great. Do everything you can to get here tomorrow."

After hanging up, Art turned to Karen. "Say, honey, what does a respectable private eye wear?" he asked.

"Depends on what kind of impression you want to make. If you're carefree, you could dust off a sombrero. A serious person would wear a dark suit and maybe a clerical collar."

"You're a lot of help. My sombrero got recycled in Buffalo along with my robes and collars."

"Maybe you're stuck with your good old dark blue suit and a few turtle necks. Take a couple of dress shirts and a tie for luck."

Art worked steadily until just after midnight, carting boxes and unneeded furniture to the garage, then cleaning up and rearranging rooms as per Karen's instructions. He nursed his tender back while he completed the work he thought necessary to have the place in decent shape for Karen to live in while he was away. He disposed of packing materials and put final touches on furniture positions while Karen made a plane reservation for Boston via Atlanta at 7:30 the next morning and arranged for a taxi to the Daytona airport.

Although she had encouraged him to take up Alan Gilead's offer to go to Boston, he had not been gone long before Karen began to miss him greatly. She wanted him to succeed in his first assignment, and, after mulling matters over in her mind, her natural curiosity became overwhelming. She decided she was going to bundle Clive up, pack a few things, and head for Boston. The right time would be in a day or two, not now, when she could surprise Art. There were a few matters to organize first, and then she and Clive could go.

CHAPTER 3

ART STOOD AS CLOSE AS HE COULD to the terminal building at Logan Airport in a not too successful effort to avoid the freezing rain that was streaming down. He shivered involuntarily, wishing he had brought warmer clothes. Poor visibility interfered with his attempts to spot Alan's car. Every time he changed position for a better view, he had to beware of the treacherous footing. Just like Buffalo, he thought. Why would bridge players want to come to Boston in late November and freeze? They could be enjoying sun in Florida, California, Texas, or heaven knew where.

Finally, he spotted a slow-moving Cadillac pulling up near the arrivals sign. The driver honked his horn. Art recognized Alan waving at him through foggy windows, and moved quickly to the car. The drive to the Westin was short, aided by firm, brief murmurs from a global positioning device that spouted occasional instructions identifying the route from the airport to the hotel. A soft voice from deep inside the little instrument piped messages like "Turn left in two hundred yards," or "Take ramp right."

"She's a big help," said Alan. "I get lost much more quickly now."

"They're remarkable inventions," said Art.

"We've been trying to make your role as challenging as possible. We managed to alienate the Boston police," said Alan.

"What happened?"

"We moved Hank's body from the spot where he was attacked. That is, the paramedics did. He was still alive, or so we thought, and we called an ambulance. The paramedics gave him a quick check and I guess they figured he was okay to move, so they bundled him up on a stretcher. He died in the ambulance on the way to the hospital. The hospital called to let us know."

"That's unfortunate. It sounds like you made all the right moves."

"I wish the homicide captain felt that way. He roasted us pretty well for moving the body."

"Sounds a little testy."

"The captain was full of grim looks and trite advice. I don't think he explained everything clearly to the coroner. The other two officers were fine with it, but the captain and coroner were upset. That may spill over into your contacts."

"Thanks for the warning. I'm not sure what to expect from the Boston police. I've never worked with them."

When they arrived at Copley Place, Alan gave his car keys to a valet, then led Art up to a conference room. The ACBL board members greeted Art and Alan as they arrived and reverted to groups of two and three, carrying on their own conversations and dissecting events of the previous day. After Alan finished dealing with his wet raincoat, he quickly took charge of the group and brought it to order.

He had taken on the position of CEO some years earlier and was skilled in the process of directing meetings with board members. He knew them all personally and had made a point of establishing friendly terms with each one. The only obstacles to his goal were a couple of hard-boiled veterans who did very little work but expressed opinions, mostly negative, on every subject brought before the board. Alan ignored them whenever possible, only smiling silently when they dropped ideas that could have led to long, futile arguments. He had learned to refrain from joining fruitless arguments and, instead, to allow other board members to destroy bad ideas.

He relayed the information that the Boston homicide detectives had been receptive to the idea of a skilled liaison man, and that Art Fraser had been everyone's choice for that responsibility. He then asked for approval of a smaller group to act as a steering committee to direct Art, and proposed a budget to cover his expenses.

Art shuddered involuntarily, partly because the cold dampness on his clothes was gradually soaking through to his skin and partly because of the term "steering committee." Signs of creeping bureaucracy did nothing to warm him. He interrupted the conversation long enough to clarify what the term meant. He insisted that he be given a free hand in the investigation and made it clear that he would put up with no interference. "A steering committee is fine as long as it helps the process. Otherwise we have a millstone. If I need help, I can contact you through Alan. I've got to be on the move twelve to eighteen hours a day. I'm sure none of you wants to stick to that kind of schedule."

Two of the board members fancied their skills as detectives and started a heated discussion about the way the investigation should be controlled. Alan was not about to have his grand plan implode so soon. He reinforced Art's message on the role he was to play and smoothed matters over by asking the two officials to talk to him personally about their concerns and leave Art free to devote his time to doing what he was paid for.

The Presidential Suite that Alan assigned to him was the largest hotel unit that Art had ever seen. Located on the thirty-sixth floor, it had great views of the Charles River and Boston Harbor. It contained a dining table with seating for eight, a built-in wet bar, two full bedrooms, three baths, a kitchen with all necessary appliances plus a separate pantry. Good quality rugs and tasteful wallpaper blended with what looked and felt like real mahogany furniture.

Art thought how helpful it would be to have a colleague with whom to work, someone to bounce ideas around with. He thought of old Stan Piper up in Erietown, New York, with whom he had worked on his last case. Stan had been a useful sounding board, even though he'd had severe limitations as a detective. Discussing progress and sorting good ideas from mere possibilities had been solid benefits of having a colleague, any colleague, to work with. It was also a satisfying part of an investigation. The more he thought about it, the more urgent the issue seemed. A person skilled in police work whom he could trust absolutely? How about Karen? She was busy with Clive, and Art was reluctant to ask her to travel with a fragile baby. Karen's background was in police work, although not in homicide, and fit this need almost perfectly. Alan had told him that Karen was welcome if she wanted to join him, and they could have the suite for the duration of the tournament. *Maybe I'll see if she wants to come up here*, he thought. *There's plenty of room for her and Clive. She'd enjoy a few days here. On the other hand, if the case goes slowly or doesn't pan out and I come under a lot of criticism from bridge players, she's sure to get hurt. There are no guarantees as to how this is going to unfold. It might be better to take the heat alone.*

The first matter on Art's mind when he finished with the board members was to establish contact with the Boston police as soon as possible. He wondered what problems he might have trying to do that on a Saturday. When he phoned, he was able to get through to the captain in charge of homicide. The captain was agreeable to having Art drop over immediately. "We've been expecting you," said Bruce Lente.

On the short trip, his cab driver was eager to talk about the disappointments of Boston football. "Last year, we ride to the top. The Giants flatten us. I could have cried. This year, our quarterback is out for the season. They play like a team of has-beens."

Although he was a sometime-fan of Buffalo, Art had little interest in the NFL and even less in the Patriots. With the Bills' season going down the drain rapidly, he had slight concern for the cabby's conversation. He had to admit though, that the cabby had an interesting philosophical perspective.

"They pay these guys so much, you know. One of their fines could buy me a couple of new cabs. I love to see them grunt when they get hit. The Giants almost killed poor old Brady last fall. Our line was a sieve. Nobody picked up on the blitz."

"I'm more of a Bruins fan," lied Art, to change the subject.

"You crazy? We got nothing since Bobby Orr and Esposito. We had Bourque for a while, and we ship him to Colorado and he wins the cup for them."

Art tuned out the rest of the monologue and was happy to see the driver pull up in front of the police station. He found the floor where Bruce Lente worked and introduced himself to the receptionist. "I'm here to see Bruce Lente."

"Oh yes. He told me to expect you. He's still busy, but won't be long."

Art accepted the coffee she offered and asked. "Lots of people around today?"

"Not a lot. But inconsiderate people still commit murders on weekends and we still need some staff around. Julia Baker is one person you're going to meet. She works for Bruce and is assigned to the case at the Westin. That's what you're here to talk about, right?"

"That's right."

In a few moments, Bruce Lente ambled over, favoring his right leg, and demonstrated a powerful grip when he shook hands with Art. Lente was wearing casual clothes, tan corduroy trousers, a white turtleneck shirt and a brown, comfortable looking sweater. His grey hair was clipped in a brush cut, a hangover from earlier days as a marine. "You're the Philo Vance of the bridge group, is that right? Over at Copley Place?" he said.

"Philo operated in New York. I don't recall him ever working in Boston. I have a contract with the bridge group, yes," said Art. "I spent fifteen years in Buffalo with the New York State Police. Five years in homicide. Then I decided to go it alone and moved to Daytona."

"Threw away your pension? You must be able to touch up your bridge guys for some big bucks. Most of us here are tied in to our pensions. Gets that way after a few years. I'm going to stick it out for another eight, hopefully."

A long-time lieutenant in the Boston police homicide squad, Lente had always been a conscientious cop. He became a minor hero in Boston after a successful raid on a drug dealer many years ago. His right shin bone had been the recipient of three bullets in the encounter and the Boston press plastered his story over its pages. For a while, he expected he would never walk again, but surgeons repaired the damage well enough so that he could get around, albeit with a pronounced limp. His effort in the case warranted a citation from the commissioner and he displayed this prominently on his desk.

The lead officer on the raid later became a superintendent in the force, and he used his influence to promote the security of Lente's tenure. Liberal high-level support provided needed assistance to Lente's career. Not many of the senior officers in the Boston police force had homicide experience. When a Lente case went wrong, few of the senior people understood enough about homicide work to decipher Lente's explanations. When Lente occasionally took a case over the brink of disaster, and his own explanations were insufficient, the superintendent's influence was there to rescue him. He managed to chug along without a whole lot of talent and with constantly diminishing effort.

As time passed, Lente's lack of political skills led first to missed promotions and then to a loss of ambition. He now avoided long hours and voluntary weekend work whenever possible. With absolutely no desire for further career advancement, he had become far more interested in family matters and his main hobby as a gardener, than in enhancing his reputation as a homicide supervisor. It was natural that, over the years, he had become a master of the shortcut in bringing cases to a head, and that he had taught his detectives how to apply his methods. His career goal was now one of hanging on for eight more years and he didn't care who knew it. He had a theory that he was still capable of rising to an occasion if a difficult case cropped up. Of course, he was not actively stretching himself to prove that theory.

When they shook hands, Art was close enough to smell a strong odor of alcohol on Lente's breath. *A little early in the day,* he thought. *Probably has a bottle in his desk drawer. Maybe a case. This is what I've got to work with. This is what the Boston public have to live with. Well, it is Saturday. Maybe that's his price for working on weekends.*

Lente introduced him to Julia Baker, the Boston detective assigned to lead the investigation. Julia turned out to be a cynical, lean woman of no more than forty. She had the potential to be very attractive, but looked as though a smile would crack her porcelain skin. Her blonde hair could have been neat, or even cut short, but bits going in several directions revealed that its owner did not care. She wore a dark, rumpled pant suit that fitted her well but had lost its shape. Art thought, *Maybe she has her dry cleaning done on Sundays.*

"You'll find Julia is one of our top detectives," said Bruce. By that he meant that he was pleased with the way Julia Baker was adopting the Bruce Lente method of homicide investigation. With almost twelve years on the Boston force and the last eight working with Bruce, Julia continually improved her understanding of Bruce's attitude towards quick dispatching of cases. He could see her leaning more and more to an acceptance of his philosophy.

Julia gave Art an unsmiling toe-to-head perusal and declared, "So you're the gent the bridge folks have hired."

"So I'm told."

"You're not from Boston? We know most of the private eyes around here."

"I spent a few years in Buffalo with the state police. I just left a short while ago and moved to Florida."

"You must be older than you look."

"Could be. I'm just getting started in my own business. This is my first contract."

"I haven't trained many greenhorns. What did you do in the Buffalo squad?"

"I didn't come here expecting to be trained. I spent several years in homicide."

Julia lifted her head sharply at this piece of news. "That's a plus."

"We had a couple of murders connected with the world of bridge—six people all together—and I was lead man in the investigations. We wrapped them all up. The bridge league thought my background would be useful. I understand your department endorsed the idea as well."

"Nice record." Art detected a slight change in Julia's attitude as the conversation evolved. He was not sure if her voice reflected a touch of respect or a touch of envy.

Art said, "I'm hoping you might be willing to share details of your investigation so far."

Lente reddened, then responded, "That's something we don't like to do. We're not required to do it. We regard our files as confidential. We pride ourselves on our work and we don't go broadcasting to the world what our suspicions are. That would only help our suspects evade us."

Art thought, *This is not my idea of an endorsement.* He said, "I know what you mean. Let's look at it this way. I'm an insider in the world of bridge. I know the people and the culture. I may be able to find things faster than someone with no involvement in that world."

Lente snapped, "I'm sure you're a very smart man, Mr. Fraser. We don't need lessons from amateurs."

Lente's words left Art momentarily speechless. *I'll bet he hasn't found a damned thing so far. I doubt that he has any idea of how much we could help each other.* Eventually, he blurted out, "Can we at least compare notes? I understand the bridge scene pretty well and may be able to help you there."

"If you have some facts for us, don't hold back."

"Please ask all the questions you want. Would you like a rundown on the way tournaments are run?"

Lente frowned. Art thought, *that seems to be his normal expression.*

"Absolutely," said Julia.

"First of all, we have this league, the American Contract Bridge League, ACBL for short. It runs all of the tournaments in North America. They organize three major tournaments each year, spring, summer and fall. These major events pretty much need the complete facilities of a big hotel in a major city. In Boston, right now, they are using the major part of two big hotels—the Westin and the Marriott at Copley Place. The ACBL rents the big ballrooms but also takes over dozens of smaller conference rooms. They need a large staff to handle the running of all the events that take place and the staff need meeting rooms and work rooms to do their jobs."

"I suppose you play for pretty high stakes," commented Julia.

"Not really," responded Art. "There are no cash prizes in North America. You might see a few side bets going on, but they're just pocket change. The real goal is masterpoints. There's a pecking order among bridge players. It's all based on masterpoints. If you have a bunch, you're high on the list. Otherwise, you could be a nobody."

"So people beat their brains out all week to win masterpoints?" asked Julia.

"That's right," answered Art. "Almost five thousand people come to play. Some play only a day or two; others are here for the whole ten days. They're mostly American but there are several from Canada and a few from Europe and Asia. They arrive at one of the ballrooms within a half hour of each other. Of that group, eight hundred of them think they're hotshots and want to play a game of bridge in the very best competition there is. They play in the national championships. The others want a good game but have no stomach for the tough competition they'd find. One of the players from each team or pair has the job of getting into a lineup to buy an entry for the competition they're entering. The take from the group playing in the national championship game would normally be between twenty and thirty thousand dollars. At this one, it was twenty-five thousand."

Julia said, "And some person or persons thought he could break the security you have in place and walk off with the twenty-five thousand."

"Right," said Art. "And created a big distraction that took everyone's mind away from that process—everyone except poor Hank and Frank, that is."

Lente replied, "That was a nice little speech. Let us know when you've got something useful."

Art had mixed feelings about his progress. Although he was encouraged by Julia's response, he felt frustrated with Lente's lack of enthusiasm and had to restrain himself. He said, "Be glad to. Let's agree that cooperation cuts both ways."

Lente asked, "Did you hear how the geniuses moved the body from the murder scene?"

Art felt himself put on the defensive once again. He remembered Alan Gilead's warning about alienation of the homicide captain. He began to think that Lente was born alienated. Right now, it seemed as though Lente was trying to antagonize him. He decided to lay on his most confident, loudest tone in talking to Lente. "I don't have all of the details. I understand that an ambulance was called and when the paramedics arrived, they gave him a thorough check and decided it was okay to move him. They took him to hospital to try to save his life."

Lente frowned, nodded, and changed the subject. "Do you have any leads at all to work on? Anything that might help us get started?"

Art replied, "I just got here this morning and had a quick briefing. I don't have anything helpful yet. Details will drift in piece by piece. If we have good contact with one another, we can share information and keep each other up to date. I'm hoping we can work closely together."

Lente replied, "Of course we'll work together. But we need a clear understanding of our relationship. Julia here is in charge of the case. She'll be your main contact with us. Think of yourself as working for her, if you like. Let me add that you would be unwise to withhold information related to the case. Any information. I'll be very disappointed if I find that we've wasted time because someone withheld important facts from us. I have, in the past, found that some private detectives like to hold back vital details in a case. I prosecuted them as accessories and I'd do the same for anyone else pulling shenanigans. Just keep that in mind."

Art's cheeks burned at these words, but he suppressed the immediate response that came to mind. He cooled down enough to ask for a few minutes with Lente alone. The man shook his head and started to mutter, but Julia eased the situation by announcing that she had a call to make and left.

Art adopted a firm tone of voice that he thought suggested there was to be no argument, no discussion about what he was saying. "I accepted a job here with the understanding that the Boston police and the bridge league were in agreement that a go-between would be a big help in solving the case. I mean someone with police experience who understands the bridge scene. I think I qualify on both counts. My only interest here is solving the case. If you don't see matters that way, why don't you excuse yourself from the case and let someone else handle it? If you want, I'll go visit Ed Davis personally and tell him what I've found."

Ed Davis was the Boston Police Commissioner, a man Art would not have recognized had he tripped over him. The name came from an article he had downloaded from the internet and studied on the plane to Boston. He reckoned that if Lente called his bluff, he lost nothing. He could just change the subject. On the other hand, dropping names had worked miracles in the past.

Lente jerked his head up at the mention of Davis' name. He muttered a few words to himself and then agreed, "Well, of course, we don't need the commissioner wasting his time on details we can handle."

"Then let's agree that we are going to work together like intelligent police officers."

"Of course."

"Call Julia and tell her I'm ready to go."

Lente went out and returned with Julia. She walked to the elevator with Art. When they were securely out of range of Lente's hearing, she said, "We recovered remnants of the fireworks that were used in the cover-up that our suspect set up. We were able to trace the name of the supplier. They have a couple of stores nearby in New Hampshire, but none in Massachusetts. They're illegal here unless you have a license. There's no way that a person planning this kind of festivity would be getting a permit."

"I agree," said Art.

"I'm going to drive up there to see them this afternoon. Tracing a customer who bought a few firecrackers will be tough. It'll be like looking for a grain of silica in a patch of quicksand, but I've got to try."

"Good luck with it. If someone bought only firecrackers, and no Roman candles or sparklers, they might stand out from the other customers. You may have some luck. There's another angle that you might check. There are products that produce smoke but no noise. You could inquire about that. There was a lot of smoke in both washrooms right after the blasts. That might help folks in the store with identification of a customer."

"That sounds worthwhile. And while we're at it, believe me, I take your point about being an insider. We really didn't know where to start on this investigation. We were going in circles. I'm totally on my own on this assignment. I don't have a partner to work with. I do need help."

"We all need help," said Art. "What time will you be back?"

"The drive up there will take over an hour, and the same back. The whole expedition will take most of the afternoon. Why?"

"I'm going to talk to some of the bridge league staff this afternoon and evening. I also want to get hold of some of the hotel staff to see what they can tell us. You might like to join me for these interviews. In any case, I can fill you in whenever we get together again."

"I could get back to the hotel by about five. Does that help?"

"If you're willing to work into the evening, we could cover some useful ground."

"Okay. See you at five."

On the way back to the Westin, Art searched his memory for occasions when, in Buffalo, he had worked alongside private investigators. The encounters had been few, and he recalled being somewhat less than impressed with their capabilities. He began to understand how the Boston police viewed him. *I think I'm getting through to Julia,* he thought. *She seems to be warming up and probably doesn't get much appreciation from her boss. Lente seems like a rotten apple. I'll have to continue a hard line with him. Not that he'll be involved much.*

~  ~

Back at his hotel, Art set about arranging to talk to all of the directors who had been present in the ballroom where the Open Pairs had been scheduled. This turned out to be a formidable task. He tracked down Fred Jardeen in his temporary office and asked about setting up a timetable of interviews. Fred had set up a work schedule for all of his staff for each event for the complete tournament. There was a break of just under three hours starting at about four-thirty each day. Art badly needed to get hold of the key people as soon as possible even if it meant interfering with Fred's preset schedule.

"I know it's Saturday, and I know it's their only break time," said Art. "We can't avoid cutting into their meal times."

Fred shook his head when he realized the times that people would be required to show up. "After the session, these people handle scoring, errors, appeals, committee arrangements, a bunch of things. Then they have to tidy up and prepare for the next session."

Art said, "We both want to see this affair solved. We can't be half-hearted about it. Here's the problem. If we don't wrap up our investigation by next weekend, the chances of catching up with the guilty party will go right down the drain. We know how quickly everyone takes off on the Monday after a national tournament. Some folks even leave on Sunday night. Everyone who can help will have left Boston. Try tracking down witnesses and suspects after the gang has left. In effect, we'll have a cold case on our hands."

"I understand what you're saying. We're going to give this absolute priority. The directing staff will all want to pitch in. I'm sure you can count on them one hundred and ten percent. But recognize that I'm running short-handed right now. Two of my best men, guys that I assign to championship events, are out of the picture. Hank is gone forever and everyone wants to see his killer arrested. Thank goodness Frank survived. He's feeling better and should be back at the tournament later this week."

"We'll need to get hold of him as well. Today, if possible."

Fred said, "That should be okay. He's really doing fine. I told him to take time off until he feels up to a full assignment. The doc is optimistic that he can come back to work as soon as he feels like it."

Fraser said, "Our first order of business ought to be a discussion with all of the staff who were around at the time of all the noise and activity Friday."

"That may be a little tough. We're talking about twelve of my most experienced directors. They're the ones I assign to work the championship events. Every one of them has an assignment laid on. If I take them all away, I shut down all of the championship events."

"We're only talking about people who were specifically assigned to the floor of the Life Masters Pairs event. We don't need staff who were working in the

Marriott, or side games in the Westin that were on another floor. Two of them were hit with darts. One we can't talk to because he's dead and the other we need to talk to separately from all the others. That leaves ten."

"True," conceded Fred. "Maybe we should split the staff into two groups."

"Why not gather them all together and get it over with? If a couple of your team have an urgent reason for not attending, I'll talk to them at some other reasonable hour. Anyone I can't talk to at a reasonable hour I'll see at an unreasonable hour. I'm available from seven a.m. until two a.m. Other times are possible."

Fred gave him a stare and nodded. "All right. You'll have to manage the time between sessions so that you can talk to all of the people you want. I'll line them up for you."

"The Boston homicide detective, Julia Baker, is meeting me at five. I'd like to meet with the group then."

"I'll give it a try. One group of ten. That sounds more reasonable. I'd better let people know that they'll have to scrap their dinner plans."

"I can't imagine it taking very long. Certainly less than an hour. I'd better take Frank's room number too. Julia and I might as well talk to him over the supper hour if at all possible. I guess we should go to his room to meet with him. We don't need to have him in the same group as the others."

"That's probably best," said Fred, handing over a note with Frank's room number.

"Another thing," continued Art. "Maybe we could post a note in tomorrow's Bulletin about the investigation. We could ask any of the players from the Life Masters Pairs to come forward if they were near the table where the robbery took place."

"As long as we give them your room number, not mine," said Fred, smiling. "I don't want eight hundred calls."

As Art finished preparing a list of questions to use in talking to the directors, he thought his next step should be to interview the hotel staff working in the area at the time of the robbery. He contacted the manager on duty for the weekend and asked for assistance in interviewing the cleaning staff. The manager told him that the housekeeping supervisor had a suite right in the hotel and might be available on short notice.

"We like to have him on hand at odd hours to deal with emergencies, so he gets an apartment as a perk. Even though it's Saturday, we may catch him there. Hang on."

Minutes later, the manager phoned back. "Chris is in. He's on his way to my office on the main floor. Come on down." He gave Art directions to his office.

Chris turned out to be a husky individual sporting a quick grin and a friendly attitude. He gave them a loud welcome when he entered the office. "I heard about all your fuss on Friday. Glad to help if I can."

Art asked, "Do you know who was on duty yesterday around the time of the robbery?"

"Oh yeah. I got a complete schedule worked out. Everybody showed up yesterday, too. Nobody played hooky. That surprised me, 'cause it seems there's always one or two that like to make a long weekend out of it. Not this time."

"Can you arrange for me to talk to your people, your cleaning staff, those who worked the ballroom area? I'd like to do that today."

"I don't know if those folks are on today, but we can give it a shot," said Chris. "Let's go to my office. I got the schedules and phone numbers up there."

Art thanked the manager for his help and followed Chris to a cramped office partly under a stairwell on the second floor. The Spartan décor reminded Art of police headquarters in Buffalo. *I hope the apartment they give him is better than this*, thought Art. Chris took a chair behind a well-worn desk, grabbed a clipboard and flipped a few sheets.

"I had two people working the washrooms where the trouble happened. Papan does the ladies' washrooms and Jose does the men's. They're both off today. They'll be in tomorrow, if you can wait."

Art replied, "I'd rather talk to them today. If I lose a whole day, I may blow my chances of solving this thing."

Chris raised his eyebrows, shook his head, muttered some numbers and made two calls. Art could hear him negotiating terms for the employees to show up at the hotel. When he put down the phone, Chris said, "I got to pay them double time plus a bit for their transportation here. This is weekend work, see. Union rules. Papan will be here at one, and Jose a little later."

"That's perfect. Thanks. See you at one," said Art.

Art was back in the housekeeping manager's office at the appointed time, and Chris introduced him to a young, pretty Mexican girl named Papan. She rose to shake hands, looking apologetic. Fraser guessed that she was barely twenty. Long black hair framed a dusky, smooth complexion, and she filled out her outfit in a superb manner. A wide mouth, thin lips and perfect teeth blended beautifully with a constant smile. She explained that she cleaned the ladies' washrooms on the ballroom floor, but unfortunately, she offered little of value about the events of Friday.

When Papan had left, Art asked Chris, "Who was cleaning the men's washrooms that day? The same thing must have happened there."

"Jose. He's the guy coming next."

Jose turned out to be a large Mexican, one of the largest Art had ever seen. He was a young fellow and, in spite of his bulk, moved easily. He had a huge black mop of hair and a tiny, drooping black moustache. Chris said something in Spanish that Art could not follow, and they switched to English.

"So you want to know something about Friday," said Jose. When Art nodded affirmatively, Jose continued before Art could explain.

"I clean the men's washroom right on time, like I'm suppose to. I never saw nobody around. Clean it all up, take the garbage out, put new towels in. Then the place blows up." He made exaggerated gestures with his arms, found the whole matter very funny and exploded with laughter.

"Are you and Papan on the same schedule?" asked Art.

"Me and Papan! Oh ho. I like to be on her schedule. What's a schedule, Chris?" Jose thought that most things he said were funny.

"You heard the explosion?" asked Art.

"Sure I did. You think I'm deaf?" More laughter.

"What actually happened between the time you put new towels in, left the washroom and you heard the explosions?"

"I got lots to do here. I don't stand around. I head for the next washroom at the other end and was going to clean it up. Then BOOM."

Art nodded, thanked him, and told Chris they were finished for now but would likely have to go back over the information later.

~  ~

When Julia arrived, Art asked, "Did you have any luck with the fireworks people?"

"Yes and no. They sold a batch of product that matched what our suspect might have bought. Several boxes of big, loud firecrackers and a half dozen smoke grenades. The clerk remembered the details because she thought that the order was unusual. Usually, if someone buys firecrackers, they get sparklers or roman candles, something with a visual impact as well as noise. They don't sell many smoke grenades."

"That sounds promising," said Art.

"True. The difficulty is that she couldn't give me any kind of description. Just a thin person in a dark coat. No specifics."

"Did he leave a paper trail?"

"Nothing," said Julia. "Paid for everything with cash. He was only in the store for ten minutes or less. Didn't browse around or anything. He knew exactly what he wanted and went directly to the clerk and ordered the stuff."

"Well, you tried. It could have been a lead."

"On with the next," said Julia.

On the way to the hotel conference room where they were meeting the directors, Art explained the format he had set up. "We're going to meet with ten of the directing staff. That'll cover everyone who was working in the ballroom at the time of the crime. I expect it will take about half an hour. Everything happened very quickly and unless some of them were right near the table where entries were sold, they won't be able to tell us much."

"I'm ready when you are."

"I've arranged for us to meet Frank Langill separately, after we've finished with the larger group. Frank is the director who survived the dart gun attack. I understand that when you were here on Friday he was pretty foggy about matters."

Julia said, "That's right. He didn't get a clear view of the person who nailed him. Just vague input like 'wore a ski mask' and 'thin guy.'"

Art had arranged for coffee and donuts. The directors came in singly and in pairs and Art introduced Julia as they entered. Nine of the staff who had supervised play in the ballroom showed up; the tenth had pleaded urgent business elsewhere. When all were seated, he started the discussion rolling. "We want to go over every detail that anyone can remember about the crime scene. Where everyone was, your perception of what happened, who you may have seen. All the details. Julia is going to ask the questions. I have my tape recorder going, and I'll keep notes as well."

"Who wants to start?' asked Julia. "It doesn't really matter because we'll come back to everyone. But please, someone—"

George Piccole spoke up. "Frank is a good friend, so let me kick off. I'm not sure what help I can be, but here are my recollections."

Julia nodded encouragement.

"Just before game time, I heard a bunch of loud bangs that sounded like gunshots. In fact, I thought for a minute that an automatic weapon was being fired. The detonations were very close together. Then I smelled smoke. It was faint, not strong at all, but it was there. A couple of minutes later the P.A. system bellowed orders to evacuate the premises. I didn't know what else to do, so I joined the flock. We gathered outside the hotel near the emergency exits. It was bloody cold out there. Boston never felt colder, I can tell you. We were all shivering. Nobody had time to get overcoats or anything warm. We were all thankful to be ordered back within a few minutes, maybe ten. We carried on with the afternoon game even though it started almost an hour late."

"Where were you exactly at the time of the robbery?" asked Julia.

"I was in the middle of the floor just getting organized with the hand records we pass out. I couldn't tell what was going on at all. Just heard noise, smelled smoke and followed instructions to get out."

The other participants had nothing to add to George's testimony. They all had slight variations on some detail, but no one had anything to add to the substance of the information George passed along. Within thirty minutes, Art invited the group to finish their coffee and adjourn. Most of the directors wanted to stick around and gossip about the whole affair. They were curious about the progress Art and Julia were making. Art hated this kind of conversation. It only led to wild rumors and he cut it off as gently and quickly as he could.

Art phoned Frank Langill and found that he was eager to talk to them. He led Julia through the passageway from the Westin to the Marriot and then to the elevator that would take them to Frank's room. On the way out of the Westin, they passed several booths where bridge-related items such as books, clothing, computer software and bridge accessories were on sale.

"It's like a small bazaar," remarked Julia.

"A very small one," agreed Art. "I never thought of it that way, but I see what you mean. The booksellers do a pretty good business. Bridge players have a thing about collecting books. Karen and I must have a few dozen. And I wouldn't part with any of them."

"Do you actually read them?" wondered Julia.

"We might not go as far as reading a whole book, but we do flip through them."

Frank Langill had his door partially open in expectation of his visitors. Art knocked, heard Frank's shout, pushed the door fully open and followed Julia inside.

Frank lay on the bed, wearing jeans, a turtleneck and a sweater. "Don't mind the stocking feet," he said. "Just taking it easy today. Back to work tomorrow, at least for a shift. Regular duty on Monday."

Julia and Art went over and shook hands. "I remember you from yesterday," he said to Julia. "You're from Boston homicide." He had seen Art occasionally at tournaments, but they did not know each other.

"How are you feeling?" asked Julia.

"Getting better," responded Frank. "I felt like I had too much wine when I first came to. Much too much. But I'm getting back to normal quickly."

"That's good to hear," said Art. "We just finished a meeting with the other directors who were in the ballroom when you and Hank were nailed. We'd like you to run through everything you can remember."

"I'll take notes," said Julia. "Please go ahead."

Frank cleared his throat. "Let's see. We were selling entries. Turnout was okay. Not spectacular. We were getting close to game time. The lineup was getting pretty short. Almost nobody left. Hank and I were just about to reconcile all the money and fill out our sheets. Then we heard this noise. It sounded like the place was being raided by a bunch with machine guns. Then the announcement blared over the P.A. system. And that's all I remember. I felt like somebody clipped me in the back of the neck. Just a quick sensation, that's all. It didn't really hurt. Then I came to. I was totally disoriented. Had to sit for a minute to figure out where I was. I was looking up at Fred. Fred Jardeen, my boss. You must know him. They had a doctor over, you know, a player who was a doctor. He just looked at Hank and me, said a few reassuring words like, you know, 'You're going to be okay', and 'Take it easy.' The paramedics got there pretty quickly, or so it seemed and they took Hank off."

Julia nodded and Frank continued, "After that, I met Julia and the other officers. I can't remember their names. I probably didn't make much sense when you asked me questions."

"You were pretty shaky," said Julia.

"I couldn't do much more, I guess. Maybe I haven't helped you much just now, either."

"Do you have any recollection of the perpetrator at all?" asked Art.

"Mostly I remember seeing a bunch of bridge players. You know, familiar faces. Nobody unusual, anyway. I do recall a quick glimpse of a figure wearing a ski mask. I didn't really get a good look. Then everything went black."

Julia and Art nodded. More probing was not going to be helpful, and they thanked Frank for his help and left.

Art phoned Karen that night to bring her up to date. She asked, "Nobody got a good look at the perp?"

"Nobody admits it so far. I've hardly started my investigation yet. Something is bound to show up. All Hank saw before he died was a person in a ski mask. Nobody was able to question him on it. He was conscious for only a few seconds before he lapsed into unconsciousness again. Frank has the same report. No description."

"Good luck. Clive is doing well. He says he knows who did it."

"Maybe you should bring him along. We could check and see if Alan will hire him."

Alan Gilead went to dinner that Saturday night with his wife and a few players who were among his best friends. He was more than a little distracted and felt his mind floating to the events of the robbery. He partially tuned out the stories his fellow bridge enthusiasts were telling. Occasional words drifted in: thirty-eight percent games they had logged that afternoon; finesses that didn't work; good luck that opponents seemed to fall into. He couldn't help asking himself whether he had done the right thing in committing league funds to a private investigator. He had acted on impulse when he learned about the robbery and listened to the Boston police fumbling their way around. At the news that a member of his staff had met with a violent death while on the job, he had become quite distressed. Perhaps he had been too emotional in his actions. The league was financially stable but not overloaded with cash, and part of his bonus depended on how well he managed expenditures versus budget. Of course, the robbery and murder were considered to be acts of god, and the board would understand that. Still, there were some members who looked at the bottom line and would think in terms of prices and budgets as they were twenty years ago. Art was positive when he quoted the fee he was demanding. It was a bit higher than Alan had assumed. Still, it would not break the bank. Not unless the case dragged for a long time. He would have to make sure that didn't happen. Art ought to be able to wrap matters up in a reasonable time. Otherwise, he had a problem. He would have to cut off the investigation as soon as the tournament ended, or certainly no more than a week later. If Art's work resulted in only dead ends, there would be a lot of egg on the face of a certain Mr. Gilead. Art was also adamant that Alan must cover all of his expenses. Alan asked, "You mean your flights and hotel rooms? That sort of thing?"

"That sort of thing for sure. But other expenses as well. For example, to cover meals, we should agree on a per diem. We need to cover taxis, phone calls, and other incidentals. Believe me, I won't rip off the ACBL. I'll just charge reasonable items. But you shouldn't expect your recently contracted private detective to cover normal expenses. If they're related solely to the case he's working on, he shouldn't have to pay for them out of his own pocket."

This was Alan's first experience hiring a private investigator and he wasn't sure what he was getting into. He had been responsible for starting the ball rolling, and there was nothing he could do to stop it now. In his favor was the fact that Art was known to a wide circle of bridge players and enjoyed a good reputation among them. How about the Boston police force? Would the homicide group take the issue seriously? He hoped so. He reminded himself that his instincts were usually reliable and should be here too.

CHAPTER 4

AT A LITTLE BEFORE EIGHT THE NEXT MORNING, Art was indulging in one of his life's pleasures. He allowed no grubby, foul-smelling electric razors in his shaving kit. Instead, he kept a collection of the latest models of blade razors, double, triple and tetra bladed, along with old-fashioned shaving soap and a very expensive, very soft brush. These were the tools for leisurely lathering his face with a rich layer of steaming soap suds, followed by carefully trimming back the last day's growth and concluding with a near scalding rinse. The clean feeling that followed was pleasant enough, and, on days when he felt he had done an especially good job, he might ask Karen to come over and supply a second opinion. Her caresses always justified the special effort, and every now and then led to an exceptional bonus.

Halfway through his shave, with a thick blob of lather on his right cheek still to be dealt with, he heard a loud, insistent knock on the door of his suite. He was indecisive about whether he could finish the final cheek when the knock came again, this time with more urgency. In the hurried process of putting his razor down, he managed a sizeable slice into the flesh on the right side of his nose. A swipe at his face with a towel dislodged half of the soap and some of the blood, now flowing freely. Art cursed silently, took one more wipe at his face, and trudged to the door.

Opening the door revealed the smiling face of Papan, the hotel worker he had interviewed the previous day. Like the others, Papan had contributed nothing of value at that time. She carried the air of a happy girl, but when she caught sight of Art's bleeding face, spotted with soap remnants, her body convulsed momentarily with the start of hysterics. She recognized the delicacy of Art's situation and brought herself quickly under control.

"Sorry, Mr. Fraser, to bother you. Maybe I need to come later?"

"No. Right now is fine."

"I just remembered something after we talked," said Papan. "Maybe you can use some information."

Art was always in the mood for evidence and welcomed the girl into the suite. It dawned on Fraser that Papan was looking for some money. *I wonder if Alan has a budget for informers. I'm glad I mentioned incidentals when I talked to him. How much is Papan looking for? I suppose I'll find out.* "I'm interested in anything you want to tell me," said Art.

"Please remember, I have a mother and two sisters," said Papan, still smiling but trying to look shy.

Here it comes, thought Art. *Probably a bunch of cousins as well.* "Tell me what you've got and I'll see what I've got."

"Not too fast," said Papan. "I think you like what I got."

Fraser sighed, excused himself and went into the bedroom to get his wallet. He returned to face Papan. "Here you go," he said, handing her a twenty-dollar bill.

Papan's hand was still out after she pocketed the first twenty. "Okay," said Fraser. "This had better be good." He gave her another twenty.

"On Friday noon hour," said Papan. "I clean the ladies' washroom like I do every hour. We got a schedule, you know. Clean them every hour. So I am in there with my sign at the door to keep the ladies out. I empty the garbage boxes and mop the floor and a guy I don't know, he comes in and replaces the paper towels. I always check them first, before I do anything and they don't need replacing. I wonder what is going on. I ask my boss later why he puts a man on to help me. He says no, he didn't put anyone else on. So. We had a fire and a big bang bang. I suppose the guy put some stuff in the garbage box to make noise and start fire."

"What did the guy look like?" asked Art.

"He wears yellow outfit, hotel outfit, just like me. We all wear the same uniform."

Nobody wears it like you do, thought Art. "Can you describe him at all? What did he look like?"

"I didn't get too good a look. Taller than me. Thin. Not a happy person. Not Mexican. White person."

"We'd better let the police know about this and get them to sketch up a face."

"I'm happy to help."

"Are you in all day?" Art asked.

"Yes. Got to work all day Sunday. Too bad."

"I'll be in touch with you later today."

Fraser took down her full name and details on how to get in touch. Papan shook hands and as she made her exit, extended her open right palm once again, smiling broadly now. Fraser produced another twenty.

When Art resumed his shave, he found that the bleeding had mercifully stopped. He lathered up once again, thumbed through his collection of razors, selected one less likely to cut nasal tissue, and finished his shave. After a revitalizing dose of orange juice, strong coffee and healthy toast with the usual berry jam, he phoned Chris to request a further meeting with Jose.

"Come on down," said Chris. "I'll get Jose for you."

Art ducked into Chris' office, greeted Chris, found a chair, and said, "I had a chat with Papan this morning. She told me about a man entering the ladies' washroom just before the time of the robbery."

"I like to chat with Papan too. Yeah, she told me about that. Asked why a guy would be in there changing towels. I never sent anyone in there. Changing towels is her job."

"Why didn't you mention all this yesterday? We were talking about what happened Friday and you didn't say a word."

"I just remembered," said Chris.

Art thought, *There's no point in getting mad. I've got to stay friends with him or I'll have even bigger problems.* He continued, "I'm going to talk to the Boston police and get them to make up a sketch of the guy she saw. They'll need her for a couple of hours."

"No problem there. I'll make sure Papan can see them."

Jose showed up, with an ear-to-ear grin as usual. At least I won't have to pay him, not in front of his boss, thought Art.

Chris said, "Mr. Fraser wants to know if you cleaned washrooms at the same time. Papan saw a guy in her washroom just before the fire."

"Lucky guy," said Jose.

"No doubt," said Chris. "Tell us if you saw anyone around the time that Papan did her work on that floor."

"I get you. Well, I clean all the washrooms on the floor where the ballroom is. I never saw nothing."

"What time did you clean the washroom?" asked Art.

"Right at the time I'm suppose to," answered Jose.

"Exactly what time was that?" insisted Art.

"Hey Chris, what time was that?" asked Jose.

"Twelve thirty is what the schedule says," answered Chris.

"Yeah, I cleaned it at twelve-thirty. Right on time."

"Don't you have a watch?" asked Art.

"Watch? What do I need a watch for? We got clocks all over the place." Jose was bubbling with laughter.

They made small talk for a while, but it became evident that whatever Jose knew, if anything, he was not disclosing it just then.

"Okay. Thanks for coming up," said Art.

After this briefest of interviews, Jose left.

Art wondered if he would hear another knock on his door in the morning, and another hand held out for a little consideration. Chris muttered, "Sometimes Jose tells you what he wants. Sometimes he tells you the truth. You got to sort them out."

"Was he telling the truth just now?" asked Art.

"My guess is no."

As Art returned to his room, he had a sinking feeling that he had made a mistake paying Papan so readily. She would spread that news like wildfire among her friends. And now he would have to pay a good, stiff price for everything he got. When he exited the elevator on his floor, he saw a large form appear from a service cubicle. The form turned out to be a smiling Jose. "Hiya, Mister Fraser. Got a minute? Maybe I got something for you."

"You remembered something," said Art.

"Of course." Jose shook with laughter. "I forgot all about it." Jose paused, waiting. Art decided to wait as well, and stood, looking Jose in the eye.

Jose's eyes moved around. His smile came and went, then came again. He appeared to summon up his courage and spoke once more. "Maybe we can make a little business deal?"

Art knew now what was coming. He laughed inwardly at himself for being a sucker. Jose, seeming to read his thoughts, started to chuckle again.

"What did you remember?"

"Let's do the business first. I am not greedy. One hundred bucks is okay."

You are not greedy at all, thought Art. *Just very good at spotting a mark.*

"That's impossible."

"Okay. Seventy-five."

"Twenty dollars now. Forty dollars if you have something useful. And if it's really useful, I will not tell Chris."

The smile disappeared completely at this.

"Oh ho. Who's Chris? Maybe I got to go. I just remembered something."

"Your memory is getting good now." Art stood his ground.

Jose seemed to waver. He turned a millimeter towards the elevator, then back, and then repeated the maneuver. Finally, he said, "Okay I seen a guy in the washroom also. Skinny guy, not too tall. He was dressed in a hotel uniform, like me and Papan."

Art mulled over the words *like me and Papan* and had to suppress a laugh as he tried to imagine a composite body made of two persons as far apart in appearance. He asked, "When did you see him?"

"I seen him a few minutes before everything breaks loose. Before the fires and the big bang bangs. I was cleaning the washroom, getting it all really nice, maybe ten, fifteen minutes before the trouble starts."

"That was probably just one of the staff using the washroom. There would be about twenty men involved. It could have been any of them."

"I tell you, Mr. Fraser, this guy did not use the washroom. He had some other business. I don't know what. This happens so close to the time when everything goes crazy. I have my sign up there about cleaning. You know, 'out of service'. Everyone else uses the other washroom. This guy just walks in; maybe he thinks he owns the place."

"Did you see him leave?" asked Art.

"No. I finish cleaning, pick up my stuff, move my sign and go to the next job. He was still in there when I left."

"Can you identify him?"

Jose found this very funny. "Maybe," he said, rubbing a thumb and forefinger together.

"The police will have to be informed about this."

Jose did not find this funny. He looked a little worried for an instant, then burst out with, "Sure. We know that. I like to help the police."

"We'll need you to work with a police artist to put together a picture of the guy."

"Okay. I might do that."

Art handed him forty dollars. Jose looked to be on the verge of tears, but when Art produced another twenty, he looked once again like his usual laughing self.

~  ~

Art had agreed to meet Julia at nine-thirty that morning and went to the lobby to join her. He was surprised to see that she was smartly dressed and had set her hair in an attractive style. He raised his eyebrows and greeted her.

"Good morning," he said, and then escorted her to the meeting room that Alan had assigned to him. "I've talked to some of the hotel staff. One of the cleaning staff—her name is Papan—saw someone suspicious in the washroom she was cleaning just before the game. The guy had no business being there. Jose— he does the men's washrooms on that floor—also had a look at the suspect on Friday. You should definitely get your artist to spend time with them and make a sketch. There may be others. We can post the picture and I'm pretty sure it'll produce a lead or two."

"Okay. That sounds solid. It won't be easy on a Sunday, but I'll try and get someone over as soon as we can. Here goes." They paused while Julia took out her cell phone and dialed headquarters to request an artist to come to the hotel. After a short wait, her phone buzzed. Art heard her say, "I'll pick him up and bring him here right after lunch."

She asked Art, "Who are the hotel folk you talked to?"

Art passed on the names and contact information of Papan and Jose. "Neither one gave me anything of value at first. They're all after money. I had to pay Papan to get information out of her and the news got around. Jose stepped up with his hand out later"

"Private operators must have a lot of loose cash. I have to be real careful with the money I hand out. We only pay trusted informers and only if they really deliver. Once people find out that easy money is floating around, their memories all of a sudden become very creative."

"I know what you're saying. Still, a lead is a lead. Maybe it'll be worth a hundred and twenty bucks. We're scratching for useful clues at the moment."

Julia said, "They'll all have their hands out now. Good luck. I'll head back to the station and pick up our artist. See you right after lunch."

"I'll line up Papan and Jose to help the artist," said Art.

Art followed up on his interview with Wendy Tetonas, a director who had been on the convention floor at the time of the robbery. Wendy arrived at Fraser's suite at 11 a.m., wearing a well-fitting track outfit. She kept herself in top physical condition by working out regularly and playing tennis on her off days. She was blessed with a perfect complexion and naturally blonde hair. Only her smile prevented her from being genuinely beautiful. Large, sharp eyeteeth and wide gaps between incisors gave her a predatory appearance. Most men thought of her wardrobe as inviting; most women called it overkill, lacking taste. In any case, she had the virtue of making few enemies and was a welcome addition to most groups. She entered the suite smiling and moved briskly to Art, shook his hand, kissed him on the lips and made sure he could feel her strong grip and firm body. Her touch quickened Art's pulse, but, remembering his status as a married man and new father, he settled for a patch of lipstick. Wendy's enthusiasm waned when she spotted the ugly, unhealed scar on his nose and she drew back.

"On my way to a workout," she announced. "You have some more questions?"

"Yes, I do. Grab a chair. You look like you're ready for a decathlon."

"I only have time for a pentathlon this morning." She smiled.

"Your phone message says you might have some information for me."

"Just a hunch about someone who's been short of money lately. I'm a friend of Phil Michaels. He's one of the directors who was on the ballroom floor at the time of the crime. The buzz is that he got into some heavy losses during the Nationals in Vegas this summer. He tried to win it back and kept getting deeper and deeper in debt."

"Did anyone have a figure?"

"Folks said over ten thousand. I don't know who mentioned the number. It came up at a dinner I had with about half-a-dozen directors."

"That would eat a big hole in the after-tax bit of a director's income."

"A big hole in anyone's nest egg, unless you're an oil person from the Middle East."

"For sure," agreed Art.

"Look, you won't be connecting my name with any of this?" asked Wendy. "I wasn't sure whether I should mention anything about Phil. He's a pretty good guy, generally. When he didn't show up for the meeting you called with the floor directors and your detective buddy, Julia, I began to wonder if Phil had something to hide."

"Of course," answered Art.

"I hope you'll be tactful in approaching Phil. Some of us know about his problem of liking to gamble, but otherwise he's solid. I can't say how true the information is about a big losing streak. Phil certainly never mentioned it."

They were interrupted by a knock at the door. Art, half expecting to see an outstretched hand attached to another member of the hotel staff, strode over to open it. He was surprised to see Karen and Clive, along with a valet carrying luggage.

"Well—" he said.

Karen instructed the valet about the luggage, tipped him, and gave her husband a thorough inspection, focusing first on the patch of lipstick and then on his scarred nose. "Not interrupting anything, are we?" she said. "We can come back later."

"I wasn't expecting you."

"That's obvious. You shouldn't pick your nose like that."

"This is Wendy Tetonas. She's a director who was on the floor at the time of the robbery. Wendy, this is my wife, Karen."

Wendy smiled brightly. "Hi Karen. Look at the little guy. Isn't he a beauty!"

At that moment, Clive made his presence felt with a loud yell and an episode of crying. Clive's genes had endowed him with a pair of lungs that would please a marathon runner and a set of vocal cords capable of drowning the output of a decent public address system. It was natural that he would make use of these assets when he was hungry, wet, frightened, or just plain ornery. His eruptions induced loving smiles from Karen, a lurch for the diaper inventory by Art, and an anxious search for a quick exit by strangers.

"I'd better leave now. Let me know if I can be of further help." Wendy completed her sentence on the far side of the door.

"Maybe I'm the one who should leave," said Karen. "You seem to have plenty of female company."

"The usual."

"That makes it fun."

"She was bringing up something interesting."

"I hate to think," said Karen, sincerely.

"Nothing solid."

"I'm glad of that."

"We were just reviewing events at the time of the robbery. You know Phil Michaels?"

"Sure."

"Wendy came across a rumor, unconfirmed so far, that he lost a pile in Las Vegas."

"Where was he during the excitement?"

"I'm going to get the low down on his activities during the robbery. Wendy and I were just discussing that when you knocked. We didn't get to finish the conversation."

"You've got a lead, at least."

"Let's call it the possibility of a lead. That rumor may not mean much. It gives Phil a motive for robbery and he certainly had opportunity. That's all. The investigation is very time consuming with no one to help me out. I find I've got to do all of the grunt work myself."

"Is the Buffalo police station looking attractive again?" asked Karen.

"Not by a damned sight. I made my decision. I mean, we made our decision. I'm not second guessing that one."

"That's my boy. How is the case coming otherwise?"

"Slowly. You know when you first get going on a case, you follow a dozen dead ends before you start to hit pay dirt."

"I got you. Do the other directors have anything to say? Or the hotel people?"

"All we're getting from them is general details. Nothing that leads to a useful thread. I've talked to the people who were actually around at the time of the robbery, but nobody has anything concrete. Believe me, I'm glad you're here. At least I can share information with you and swap opinions. Working by myself has its frustrating moments. I'm used to bouncing ideas around with the guys."

"Too bad about the guys. I can't help you there. Anyway, I won't hear much with little noisemaker going at it."

"Has Clive been bad that way?"

"Not at all. I don't think he'll bother us. He hollers when he's hungry and when he needs a change. Otherwise, he's fine."

"Good. Apart from my lack of progress, I'm having a hell of a time with the homicide captain. He's over the hill and he thinks he doesn't need any help. He should be retired."

"You'll manage. You're good at handling tough guys."

Art's words helped Karen to recover from her attack of jealousy and she involved herself in examining their temporary accommodation. Art showed her around the suite and helped her get organized in the bedroom. "This is luxurious," she said. "I've never stayed in a hotel suite before. The furnishings are lovely. And look at the view."

"Boston in the winter," said Art. "Reminds me of Buffalo."

"Nothing is that nice," quipped Karen.

"It's a surprise to see you," said Art. "I thought you were staying home."

"I was getting lonely."

"I'm happy to see you."

They were interrupted by a phone call from the concierge announcing the arrival of a police artist. Art suggested that Karen order a crib from the housekeeping service and left Karen to settle herself and Clive. In the lobby, he spotted a young man hovering near the concierge desk. Dressed casually in jeans and a leather jacket, he carried none of the trappings that Art expected: neither paper, brushes, nor pencils. Instead, he had a large laptop bag slung over his shoulder. He introduced himself as Joe Karsh when Art explained who he was.

Art took him up to the floor where he had a meeting room assigned. He called Chris and asked to have Papan and Jose sent down right away. While they were waiting, Joe offered to demonstrate his software. Art quickly agreed. Joe plugged in his laptop and turned it on.

"You look surprised," said Joe Karsh with a smile. "I cut and paste facial pieces and body parts together using software. Hair, cheeks, nose, teeth, ears. The CIA and the FBI use the same product. I've got thousands of facial features on my machine—racial characteristics, hair features, and facial markings like piercings, moles, scars, you name it. Hats, different glasses. It used to take a whole day to put together a decent sketch. I can do one now in a couple of hours, plus interview time. I can ship my pictures around, too, if I ever need to share with another police department in another city."

"That's impressive," said Art. "How are your results?"

"They have gotten better and better over the last couple of years. They'll never be perfect. When you compare some of my sketches with photos of actual perps, the results are laughable. But I've had some real successes. It depends a lot on the witnesses. If they had a good look at the suspect and have a good eye for detail, we can really click. The worst witnesses make up details or don't remember clearly. You have everything in between. Most detectives in Boston now won't be without a sketch if it's at all possible."

Chris appeared at the door of their meeting room with Papan and Jose in tow. "Here you go," he said and left immediately. Joe's eyes widened when he saw Papan. They shook hands and he said a few words in Spanish. She giggled and sat down with him. He greeted Jose and showed him a chair. Art lingered while Joe explained the process he was going to lead them through, and then he left them together. When he returned an hour later, he was surprised to find Julia Baker sitting with Papan, Jose and Joe. The four were discussing a picture on Joe's screen.

"Look like anyone you know?" asked Julia.

"Vaguely," said Art. "I'll have to look at it some more."

"I'll take a copy," said Julia.

"Were Papan and Jose helpful?" Art asked Joe.

"Sure. I got as much as I could from them."

"Am I done?" asked Papan.

"You don't have to go," protested Joe, and addressed her in Spanish once again. Art knew enough of the language to understand that Joe was suggesting that he had an urgent need for a refresher course in Spanish. The conversation generated musical laughter, a radiant smile, and a set of dimples from Papan.

"Stick around for a few more minutes," said Art, addressing both Papan and Jose, who followed Art's directions and sat down. Art and Julia studied Joe's screen for several moments. At first glance, the figure bore a moderate resemblance to Phil Michaels.

A lean person of medium height, with eyes glowering out from under faintly colored eyebrows, and a neatly combed head of short, thick, blond hair brought Phil to mind right away. No jumping to conclusions, thought Art. We have to work this through.

As he studied the composite picture, the differences from Phil's appearance became clearer and clearer. Phil's brows were bushy. He had a square jaw, but his nose had a trace of a bulb at the end and was not symmetrical. That gave the impression of a somewhat clownish appearance. When you talked to Phil, the impression of a clown faded rapidly because Phil seldom smiled. When he did, he exposed a set of teeth with noticeable coloring somewhere between yellow and brown – a dull orange that marked a man who didn't own a toothbrush or hadn't taken lessons. Could Joe pick up this kind of detail? He would have to talk to him some more. Joe's creation thus far did not capture the nose and teeth that characterized Phil's appearance so clearly.

"What's your next step?" Art asked.

"I'll print this off in color as best I can, show it to Papan and Jose, get their final comments, and then make adjustments to get it as close as we can to the real face. That's as far as I can go without more input."

"How much detail can you pick up?"

"What kind of detail?"

"I am thinking of teeth. Are they spread apart? Perfect? Decayed? That kind of thing."

"I have about fifteen different types of teeth that I show to witnesses. They only help if the suspect smiles a lot. Teeth don't usually show up. Sometimes they can make a connection. I mean one set will often trigger a memory. Depends on the habits of the suspect. Does he keep his jaw shut tight? Does he have an habitual facial expression? Neither of your witnesses gave me information on the teeth. Do you think it's important?"

"Yes. It could be very important. We might clear one suspect if we had a positive comment on teeth. The guy I am thinking about has totally discolored front teeth. If Papan or Jose saw good teeth, it would take the heat off of him. Or vice versa."

"I'll run the teeth issue by them and build their comments into the finished draft. You can take another look then."

Papan and Jose understood little of this exchange and were getting restless. Art asked them if they had noticed anything about the suspect's teeth. It turned out that neither of the pair had noticed anything helpful.

When Joe had wrestled final comments from the pair and added final touches to the composite, he saved the picture of the face he finally decided on and printed off copies for Julia and Art. Julia took hers directly to police headquarters to discuss with her boss. Art went to the Bulletin editor with a request to have the composite plastered on the front page of the next day's edition.

CHAPTER 5

THE BULLETIN EDITOR CAME THROUGH with his promise to insert a half-page composite picture on the front page of the Monday morning Bulletin. The remainder of the front page covered details of the crime, an obituary of Hank with a picture, and a request for anyone with information to call Art's number.

When Julia showed up for their morning meeting, Art showed her the Bulletin picture. She took a quick look and asked, "Any further along in getting him identified?"

"There's a suggestion that one of the league staff members – a director – has a resemblance. I haven't checked it out myself yet." Art flipped open his notebook and recounted the highlights of the interviews he had completed. "I expect to hear from a few more people today. The guy we're talking about is rumored to have lost a wad of money in Las Vegas. That was where we held our big tournament in the summer. His name is Phil Michaels."

"Where was he at the time of the robbery?"

"He was assigned to the championship event, working on the floor where all the problems took place."

"I thought we talked to all of the staff working that event."

"We talked to nine of them. The tenth didn't show. That was Phil Michaels."

"How come we haven't talked to him since?"

"All the reports were beginning to sound like a broken record. I thought he'd have nothing to add."

Julia mulled this over for a few moments. Then she said, "I need to talk to him."

"I have the same idea. Michaels is certainly one of the people we should talk to. Let's do that together."

"We'll see how our schedules fit."

The little ice age is returning, thought Art. *She's peeved because I overlooked follow-up with Phil.*

Julia continued, "This guy you're speaking of, Phil Michaels. Can we go get him right now?"

"He may be working a shift at the moment. I'll track him down and set up a meeting. I can call you as soon as I get him," responded Art.

"Hell, if he's in the building, let's talk to him. We don't need to wait all day to get to one witness."

Art tried to reassure her. "If we interrupt a game, we'll make enemies of all of the directing staff. We'll have about a hundred players cheesed off as well. Phil is not going anywhere. He has a job to do and he's needed every minute. We're much better off to see him when he's off duty."

"I don't see that. What if he disappears?"

"Very unlikely. If he were going to disappear, he'd be long gone by now."

"I'll have to take your word for it this time. I'd like to get a photo of this guy Michaels to compare with the composite. How could I do that?"

"I'm pretty sure I can get one for you. Hang on." Art connected to the room where the Bulletin editor had his office, found that he did have a photo of Phil Michaels in his computer, and was willing to print it off right away. Art took her down to the Bulletin office and arranged for her to pick up the photograph.

Julia opened her briefcase, took out the artist's preliminary composite picture and made a quick comparison with the photo she had just acquired. She raised her eyebrows. The match was superficially close. She stuffed everything away and headed for the parking lot. Before leaving the Westin, she made a point of getting a receipt for what she considered Boston's outrageous parking fees, and then drove to police headquarters.

When Julia arrived in her boss's office, she set her briefcase down, wrestled off her trench coat, and greeted him. "Hey Bruce. Keeping warm?"

"I like to leave the fresh air to fresh young folks. It's only a few degrees below freezing. Makes your cheeks rosy."

Julia blushed to an even deeper red.

"So. You arrested the perp and you want me to call the D.A.'s office."

"That would be nice. Except that the perp is unknown so far. But let me show you this."

Julia took out the composite picture and laid it on Bruce's desk. She then set beside it a photo that she had obtained of Phil Michaels. "What do you think?"

"They'll never make the Celtics," said Bruce.

"I mean the resemblance. It's awfully bloody close."

Bruce took a closer look at the two, and agreed. "There are definite points of similarity. The shape of the head. The short hair. Very close."

"This guy lost a bundle in Vegas over the summer."

"So?"

"You can see the resemblance to the artist's picture. And he had a motive. He needed money. He was right there on the spot at the time of the crime, so he had the opportunity. He's an insider who knows the system—all the key facts. How money was handled. How much there would be. How to get at it. How to get out of there with it. This certainly looks to me like a job by an insider. This guy has all the qualifications he needs for the job."

"Says who?"

"I'm getting useful stuff from our friend Fraser."

"Our friend?'

"You introduced him to me on Saturday."

"I'm well aware of that," said Lente. "But we don't want to share any credit with private detectives, do we?"

"I'm not sure what you mean."

"I mean, we're going to solve this case, if humanly possible, and do it quickly. We gain nothing by sharing credit with private investigators. They're generally a big pain."

"But he is, was, I mean, a good cop."

"And?"

"Okay. We certainly don't have to organize the investigation his way."

"That's what I like to hear. Now, let's go back to the guy you're suspicious of. Does anyone know exactly where he was at the time of the attack?"

"He was there, working in the ballroom, right at the crime scene when hell broke loose. He was one of the officials at the event. He would have worked eight hours a day. Sometimes twelve. Directors usually have a session off every couple of days. Everyone, all of the officials and a lot of the players, stay there for the whole twelve days of the tournament. Not only that, but when we called a meeting to interview the staff running the big event, one person skipped the meeting. Guess who."

"This guy?"

Julia nodded affirmatively.

"Maybe we do have enough on him. I wonder if we're ready to arrest this guy. We need another nail to close the coffin. Can you tell me anything else? Does your suspect know anything about these dart guns? Does he have any history of using them or even knowing about them?"

"I'll look into it."

Bruce nodded approval, then continued, "Your first step should be to search his room. Maybe bring him in. We'll need a warrant. I'd like us to talk to the D.A. Let's find out what the D.A. wants."

Julia sat quietly for a moment. Then she said, "I can get it rolling this morning."

"I'd like to see you do that. And I'd like to move quickly."

Throughout the morning, Fraser received a steady flow of phone calls from players who thought they were close to the scene of the robbery and killing, or thought that perhaps they could identify the person in the picture. A few more came in during the afternoon game. He kept track of all of the respondents and made appointments with each to meet in the conference room he was using as an office as soon as possible. Some were able to come up immediately. Fraser laid out a copy of the Monday Bulletin for easy reference. During the interviews, he questioned each of the informants carefully on all of the facial characteristics in the picture. Most of his visitors backed off in their assertion that the resemblance was close, and concluded the discussion with a recognition that the person they had in mind was too old, had a smaller nose, or ears that didn't match the face on the Bulletin at all. Two of the informants stuck to their guns, and Fraser gathered what personal data he could. Shortly after four-thirty, the remaining informant volunteers began to show up. Fraser repeated the process he had used with the first group, and was able to compile names of four people who possibly matched the appearance in the composite picture.

Every single one of the respondents wanted to tell the same story. It seemed as though they had memorized a scene from a play. Noise, smoke, concern, panic, evacuation of the building, a thankfully brief interlude in the freezing cold on a sidewalk, a return indoors and finally a game of bridge. Not a one had noticed anything of material use to the investigation. The perpetrator had kept a low profile during the whole affair, and became active only when people's attention had been totally diverted to the fireworks.

When the talks concluded, Art phoned the numbers that the players supplied. His first contact was at home, living in Alabama and had no plans ever to play in Boston. The second was at home in California, enjoying the weather. The other two were reported to be in Boston for the tournament. He went down to the ACBL registration desk where all players attending the tournament were invited to register their names and temporary addresses in return for a handout containing information about the city and a few trinkets. The players he was seeking were staying at the Westin. He was not surprised to find them out of their rooms, and he left messages for them to get in touch. They called over the supper hour and expressed delight at an opportunity to drop up to talk to Art.

The first arrived in an electric wheelchair. The final prospect had a superficial resemblance to the picture, but no one would ever classify a two hundred and ten pound man as thin. Art chuckled inwardly, remembering how he had focused on facial characteristics during his interviews and not discussed other physical features.

At the end of the process, he was back to the beginning.

When Art had got hold of Phil and arranged a lunch hour meeting in a small conference room adjacent to the playing area, he phoned Julia to give her the details. "That was fast," she said, sounding surprised.

"He's on duty at one, and I promised him we'd be done by noon, so we don't have much time."

"Be right there," said Julia.

Art went down to the meeting room and set up the furniture to his liking. Phil showed up a bit early, just as Art was finishing. "You'd have no trouble getting a job as a setup man with the hotel," said Phil. "All that muscle. All that initiative."

"I've been practicing. Maybe I should get an application in," said Art. "I hear the pay is good here."

"Furniture management in the mornings. Investigations afternoons and evenings."

Julia popped in during this exchange and Art introduced her to Phil. He wanted to keep Phil at ease so that the questioning would go smoothly. "How's the attendance been at the tournament?" asked Art.

Phil responded, "Crowds haven't been affected by the robbery, if that's what you mean. Our table count seems to be decent so far, but not great. People don't like to change commitments unless there's a real disaster. Once they have plane and hotel arrangements booked, it's a real pain to make changes. Fall Nationals are never huge. Boston never compares with Orlando or San Francisco. Summer Nationals at a place like Vegas or Toronto always outdraw a site like Boston, especially Boston in the fall."

"What are you up to today?"

"I'm working the board-a-match team game this afternoon. Those events aren't all that popular anymore, but it's a premium event and I expect a decent crowd."

"Some would classify Friday as a disaster. You were on the playing floor at the time?"

"I was there. It took us almost an hour to quiet things down and get the game moving. Listen, I want to apologize for being a no show at your meeting on Saturday with the other directors. I had an appointment I couldn't miss. I thought we could catch up later anyway."

"That's okay. You can bring us up to speed right now. What was going on just before the game, while entries were being sold?"

"We don't do much during the entry sales. If we're not selling, we just hang around and direct traffic. We were getting ready to roll when everything hit the fan."

"What exactly were you doing when the place erupted?"

"Like I said, just directing traffic. We have more than one lineup of people buying entries to the event, and some folks don't know exactly where to go to buy them. We direct them to the lineup for the open game or for the flight-B players. Team games are held in a different room, and we give people directions. Then, they get their entries and they have simple questions about which section is where. It's a form of babysitting, really."

"You mentioned Vegas. I take it you were there this summer. And you had good crowds?"

"Vegas always draws well. You go there in the summer when the temperature is a hundred and twenty and people still flock there. They love it. The bars, the casinos, the restaurants, they're all fun and all reasonable."

"You'd go there anytime?"

"You bet. Mind you, I lost my shirt this year."

"How much was your shirt worth?" asked Julia.

"I lost about fifteen thousand. Not quite that much, maybe."

"Are you a good player?"

"I'm okay at blackjack. I can play poker, but I'm not as good as the real pros. If you get a couple of really good pros in a poker game, you can forget about winning. You don't know who they are when you sit down, and they just surprise you. They clean you out."

"So you just play blackjack?"

"That's it."

"How come you lost so much if you're a good player?" Julia continued her questions.

"Hard to say. I know I started to make some bad decisions. The thing is, they felt like good decisions at the time. I have certain rules that I go by, and I never break them. At least I try not to. I was probably a little tired and not focusing the way I should. I chalk it all up to a run of bad luck. I'm ahead overall in spite of the Vegas fiasco."

"That amount of money doesn't bother you?"

"It certainly does bother me. But I don't sit around moping. Like I say, I'm ahead overall. I'll get it back. I'll make sure I'm well rested next time."

"So losing fifteen thousand is no great concern?"

"Nobody likes to drop that much. I've made up my mind to forget it. I win regularly. Once in three or four times I might have a losing session. This is the biggest loss I've had, ever. But I've won more than that a couple of times. Stay cool, that's my motto. Believe it or not, it doesn't hurt to lose occasionally. The casino staff don't like players with a perfect winning record. They often get invited to leave."

They thanked Phil and he left at that point.

"He seems to be in control," said Art. "He was certainly open about his record. I didn't sense any effort to hide anything."

"That would depend a little on how much practice he has had in telling lies. I've seen some pretty good liars."

"Yes. There are some smooth ones out there. But I'll say this for Phil. He looks you in the eye and doesn't hesitate with answers. I don't get the sense he's making up a story. He talks openly about his mistakes. Everything he says seems to check out okay. He talks about big swings in winnings and losses. Other good blackjack players I've talked to are much steadier. They tend to win consistently. That is, until the house gets on to them, and invites them to never come back. I know a few bridge players in that category. Guys that the Hilton, for instance, won't allow in their casinos."

"Because they win too much?" asked Julia.

"That's right. Consistently. One of the guys is in his nineties. Not welcome."

"Really? Are you any good at blackjack?"

"Terrible. No interest," responded Art. "I borrowed a couple of books once. It seemed that each one gave you two hundred pages of solid, unconnected details to memorize. My mind doesn't work that way. Bridge has a logic to it. It doesn't seem like memory work, somehow. You can always go back to basics and figure a problem out."

"And poker?"

"Poker has a small technical element. In that sense, it's the opposite to bridge, as a card game. You have to have a good feel for percentages. But ninety percent of poker is about reading the habits and mannerisms of people at the table."

"And you don't have to do that at bridge?"

"It helps, to some extent. Maybe one hand in fifty. But truly successful bridge players have great technical ability."

"But not memory work?"

"A good memory helps, no question. But the ability to reason logically is the key. You can win in the short run without it, but the consistent winners of big events have that ability in spades."

"Interesting. Are you a logical thinker, like the other great bridge players?"

"I try. Don't think of me as a great bridge player. I'm closer to a novice. Bridge players spend years learning technical aspects of the game. Just when they think they've learned them all, they find they have to learn the exceptions. That's the edge the great players have—recognizing exceptions to the norm."

"How humble you are."

"More like a realist. Tens of thousands of players know the rules. Maybe a hundred really understand the exceptions."

"Getting back to our buddy Michaels, we'd better keep tabs on him."

"He doesn't seem to me like a man in a hurry to go anywhere. I sense that he's not going to rush off. If he goes anywhere, we know where to find him. He agreed readily to our meeting today and showed up in good time. There's an outside chance that he was involved, but we ought to just continue talking to some of the other directors. There has to be someone who knows something useful. I'd like to compare notes with you after you've talked to a few more. And there's the hotel staff. You've met Chris, the housekeeping boss, and Papan and Jose. Those are the people who might help us. We may get more out of other hotel employees as well."

Julia frowned as Art spoke. He could sense that she got her back up when someone told her what to do. *She doesn't even like suggestions. Accepting the notion that I could be a real help to her seems to be a struggle. And I'm pretty sure she won't tell me everything she comes up with. Probably her boss is influencing her. It's going to be tough to get the idea across to these Boston people that we all gain by cooperating.*

"Have all of the directing staff had a good look at our composite picture?"

"I believe they have. The most important persons to question about the picture are the dozen we interviewed Saturday. They were close to the crime scene. We'll show them our picture and make doubly sure that they take time to study it and have a chance to comment."

On the drive back to the police station, Julia reflected on the course of the investigation. At her first meeting with Art, she had approached their relationship with her usual disdain, but, as they worked together, she was beginning to realize that he was a talented investigator.

Her father had been a small-town policeman in western Massachusetts, with a never-fulfilled ambition to join the FBI. He'd instilled this ambition in his daughter's mind, unsuccessfully, as it turned out. After taking a law degree without distinction, she took the training that the FBI had to offer. Many of her classmates dropped out along the way, but Julia battled her way through. After final interviews with the teaching staff about a first assignment, she concluded that the stressful life with no real personal time was not for her. She applied for a position on the Boston force, asking for a homicide assignment. Four mostly unsatisfactory years patrolling a beat with various male partners finally led to the job she wanted. Or, thought she wanted. She came under the influence of Bruce Lente. Her dream had been that, working alongside Lente, she would learn a great deal about homicide investigations and would observe first hand how an enthusiastic leader operated. Bit by bit, the dream was shattered. She found no signs of enthusiasm. She learned little in the way of modern homicide techniques. Instead, she learned the Lente system of investigation. *Be quick to arrest. Get all the publicity possible. Let the lawyers work out the details.* A cynical streak in her character expanded and spilled over into her personal life. Mediocre results followed mixed results. The vibrant, attractive young girl lost ambition, lost interest in her appearance, and switched her focus to instant gratification of material desires.

There were a few detectives with whom Julia truly relished working. Bill Steele was one. Steele was an experienced detective, probably the best at their station, and almost certain to take over as head of their homicide group when Lente retired. Added to all that, she and Bill were good friends. Bill's enthusiasm for casework never flagged. He never took shortcuts, and was always thorough in sifting through details of apparent evidence. Although he had been mired in the bureaucracy of the police force, he remained true to his own standards and stayed absorbed in his work. Julia would have liked to work with him much more frequently, but that did not pan out. She hardly ever got an assignment with him. Perhaps Fraser was cast in the same mold as Steele—bright, honest, and full of energy. That was the type of person she had wanted to work with from the beginning. The thought energized her as she mulled over the assignment.

Karen asked, "How's the response to the composite picture you plastered on the Bulletin? Any luck there?"

"Here," responded Art, showing her the front page of the Monday Bulletin. "We've asked anyone with the faintest possibility of a scrap of evidence to contact me, or Alan Gilead, or any director."

"And everyone is lining up to talk to the big detective," said Karen.

"I'm not sure what you mean by 'the big detective'. But there certainly is a lineup. I got about a dozen calls in response to the Bulletin picture. I'm expecting some more this afternoon. We also asked for anyone to come forward who might have been near the director's table where entries were sold. I got a couple of leads to follow up on, but they all fizzled. I need a different approach. I think I should cool off my efforts to get information through the players. So far, that's been a big time waster. Everyone wants to gossip. If there's a single physical characteristic resembling our picture, some of the respondents claim they've seen a match. One guy came up in a motorized wheelchair. His hair matched the picture though. I'll say that."

"Nobody could pass on any useful information?"

"When I questioned them closely, most of them realized that the picture didn't resemble the person they had in mind."

Karen mused, "You'd think somebody, one of the players or directors, would've seen the perpetrator, or seen something that would help to identify him."

"Not so far. Julia and I are going to show the picture, personally, to all of the directors on the floor at the time of the robbery. That's our next step."

"That's about all you can do. Something will break," she reassured him.

"We need to contact the outfit that sells those immobilization guns. There aren't too many of them around. One big one. Chances are the perp ordered it over the internet and we may be able to trace it."

"How big are those things? The dart guns, I mean."

"There are two kinds. One is revolver style, the other a rifle. They're full-sized versions. Bulky. The revolver style isn't small. They use either compressed air or an explosive cartridge. I assume the air version was used here, since it's much quieter. If a couple of cartridges were fired, someone would surely have heard them."

"If it's the size of a big revolver, the perp had to have some place to hide it. Even a good shoulder holster doesn't completely hide a revolver under a jacket."

"Good point there. The perp might have been wearing a jacket. He'd need something to conceal one of those weapons. It's not like a derringer, something you could strap on a leg to hide it."

"What about a big fanny pack?" asked Karen.

"It'd have to be pretty big. That's possible, though."

"I've seen some pretty big ones. A big fanny pack would stand out. A loose jacket might do it also. Not that many people dress up. You could probably name most of them right now. None of the directors wears one."

"I guess that's right. They all wear a jersey with their name on it. No jackets anymore. As for a fanny pack, I guess we could ask around about anyone wearing an unusually large one. We have a good chance of tracing the gun through the supplier. We have the name of the company supplying the darts. Chances are the gun was bought from them as well. We'll need to contact them as soon as possible."

"I can look into that. I've got time on my hands while we're here. Clive sleeps most of the time and it'll give me something to do when he's asleep. Once we know who all the purchasers were, we can compare them to an ACBL database of names. That might get us somewhere."

"Terrific. That would be a real help. It'll give me more time to visit the directors. I ought to talk to somebody about the ACBL database of players. Maybe I can find something there. Certainly if you come up with some names from the dart supplier, we might be able to get someone run a comparison. It'll be worth digging into."

"We're off," said Karen.

When Art returned later that afternoon, Karen looked happy. "I've got something interesting," she chirped.

"Lay it on me," responded Art.

"First of all, I found a good contact at the company that supplies these dart projectors."

"Projectors? We were talking about a pistol."

"Right. Maybe wrong. I had a talk with this lady in Pennsylvania. Her name is Marge. I told her what we're doing and she says a pistol wouldn't be an ideal weapon for the job. If you buy a pistol to fire these darts, you have limited options. They don't make miniatures. A dart pistol is almost fifteen inches long and it's fat. How could you hide a thing like that? There's no silencer available. You have nowhere near the selection you find in revolvers. And these pistols aren't made for rapid firing. You shoot one dart and then you have to stop and reload. Get another dart out of your pocket, load it up and shoot again. They're not six shooters. You might say they're one shooters. So you have to carry two of them if you want to deal with two people in a short time."

"What else could a perp possibly use? A rifle would be even harder to hide."

"Who said anything about a rifle? She says we ought to look at a blowgun. They're small, thin, easy to hide. Obviously very quiet. They're sold in pairs. Our perp could have come in with a loaded pair, and when the scene was right, pulled them out one at a time, blown his darts and scooped up the money."

Art thought this over for a moment and then conceded, "You may have something there. Blowguns. I thought they were used in Africa by the natives."

"A lot of cultures have used them. Indigenous tribes mostly. The rain forest tribes in South America are the best-known users. Cherokees as well. They were good for hunting small game, not for fighting. But nowadays, a lot of veterinarians and zoo workers also use them."

"You sound like a professor."

"You should hear Marge talk about them. She could write an encyclopedia. Anyway, the person we're after must have been able to get within a foot or two of the target. At that distance, a short blowgun, probably only two feet long, would deliver a dart accurately and forcibly enough to immobilize a man. It would take a little practice, but Marge says that a trained person could easily do it."

"Did Marge give you an idea of the size of these blowguns?"

"She says they're about as thick as a fat pen. They vary from about two feet long to six feet, depending on how far you want to shoot the dart. In our case, the distance would be very short, so a two-foot pipe would do the trick. They certainly wouldn't take up much room."

"So they could easily be hidden in a sock."

"Hidden anywhere. A sock is a possibility. A jacket of any kind would conceal a pair quite easily. An inside pocket on a pair of trousers would do the job nicely."

"So where does that take us?"

"Marge is going to help me track down the names of people who bought blowguns. Their biggest volume items are rifle-type projectors. Revolvers are much smaller, and very few blowguns are sold. It'll take a few days, but she says it'll be a short list."

"That's good work. Keep the heat on your friend."

"I wouldn't dream of it. She had no reason to lift a finger. She was very cooperative—volunteered all of this information and she's going to send me the names of buyers. You won't keep people like her on board by putting heat on."

A subdued Art changed the subject. "I wish more people were as forthcoming as your contact. I started something by paying Papan for information. Now all of the staff have their hands out when they see me."

"We all learn," laughed Karen.

Art found that he couldn't go anywhere without people stopping him and asking him questions about the case. He hated saying that he had no comment, but he was in no mood to speculate about his meager findings with anyone except Karen. Any facts or ideas he talked about would be sure to start a raft of rumors. He touched base with Alan Gilead late in the afternoon, and summarized the status of the case. They discussed the money involved.

Alan said, "Our records show that there was close to twenty-five thousand dollars involved. A little under twenty percent of that would be in bridge bucks and checks, and the balance in cash."

"You're saying that there was roughly twenty thousand in cash plus the rest. Can we get the serial numbers of the bridge bucks?" asked Art.

Alan thought this over. "We sell bridge bucks only at national tournaments. Each issue starts with a new sequence. Personally, I'm not using any right now, so I can't tell you the serial numbers that we're using in Boston. But I can find out the starting number for the bucks used in Boston easily enough. People tend to buy several days' supply when they make a purchase, but the lower numbers for sure would be the ones in circulation Friday. We have records of all of the bucks sold on the first day of the tournament. Those will be the ones we're interested in."

"Let's get the numbers then. If any of those bills did show up, we'd have something to go on."

Alan said, "It'll be tricky. Directors can hardly check the serial numbers of all of the bridge bucks as they take them in."

Art responded, "Let's get the information though. I don't want to overlook any possibilities. I realize that it may be just coincidental even if we do come across some of these bills circulating. But it might not be. And we may be able to do some fingerprinting."

Alan phoned the business office and asked for Henry Katz, the director who normally had charge of bridge buck sales. He quickly got the starting serial number and the dollar amount of sales on Friday. Art made a note of the information.

Art said, "What I'd really like to do is to search the rooms of all of the directors. Someone may have a stash of cash, or the murder weapon, any of the props that were used in the killing."

"We've got maybe fifty directors on site," responded Alan. "I suppose the D.A. and the detectives on the case could authorize a search. I certainly can't."

"I know. I was thinking out loud. What we have to do now is to make sure all of the directors, or at least the ones selling entries to the games, have this list of serial numbers at hand. They can check to see if any of these bucks show up."

Alan agreed to set it up with Fred Jardeen.

CHAPTER 6

LATE THAT AFTERNOON, Julia appeared at the Westin manager's office, showed her warrant, obtained a pass key and got directions to Phil Michaels' room. She had the desk clerk phone first to make sure no one was in. The room was neatly made up and everything was stowed away carefully. Julia slipped on her latex gloves and carefully inspected every drawer, cupboard and closet in the room. She found nothing in a suitcase, but a smaller bag, the size of a carry-on, had a side pocket containing a large wad of money. Julia took a rough count, splayed them, set her digital camera on macro and took a few photographs of the roll of bills. She put everything back and left the room.

Knowing that Bruce Lente would not be at his desk after five, Julia drove home instead of returning to the station. She downloaded the pictures onto her computer and printed off color copies of the photos on plain paper. They turned out surprisingly well. Then she called Bruce at his home.

"I had a good look through Michaels' hotel room. He had a pile of money stored in a bag. I'd say at least five thousand dollars. Odd that he would carry that much cash around. I got pictures. Good pictures."

"Okay," said Bruce. "Have you called the D.A. to fill him in?"

"That's my next step."

"Okay. Get a feel for where he wants to go with this."

Bert Orchnay, the lawyer from the district attorney's office assigned to work with her, was normally helpful, but turned out to be skeptical when Julia told him details of the case. "What you've got is good, Julia. But any case you could put together is full of holes. Can we pin down anything else? How about bringing him in for serious questioning? Maybe probe his story and look to arresting him later."

"If we bring him in for questioning, we put him on the defensive right away. He'll be watching every step from then on. If we can put together a solid case for an arrest, we have him off guard."

"I hear you. But what's solid so far? How about a murder weapon?"

"I don't have one."

"Do we have a reliable witness who saw him perform?"

"We don't have one of those, either."

"Can you find any link that shows he was familiar with the type of weapon? Anything in his background that tells us he knows how to use dart immobilizers? If not, you'd better just bring him in for questioning. I'll process a warrant for that."

"Okay. Fax it over and I'll bring him in tomorrow." She called Bruce again to let him know.

"I'll come with you tomorrow and we'll pick him up together. I'll get in touch with my friend at the GLOBE. He may want to come around for a story."

Eight years of apprenticeship with Bruce had taught Julia that at times he would act on impulse in ways that no one would expect of a veteran homicide officer. She realized she shouldn't have been surprised at him barging in. If an investigation was being carried out within the "Lente" rules, he generally kept his hands off. But when an investigation reached a point where some favorable publicity might be possible, the rules changed. He could move right in. He knew how much the police hierarchy smiled on positive publicity. Nothing would beat a photo op with a suspect in tow.

Karen and Art discussed the case that night over a meal of frozen dinners heated up in their microwave. The mixture of overcooked chicken, where it could be found, and soggy pasta did nothing to improve Art's mood. Karen ignored the food in her excitement over her success in tracing the supplier of darts, and the possibility of linking a blowgun buyer with a suspect.

"If we got a hit there, it might break the case." She beamed.

"We're a long way from breaking the case, but the thread certainly has possibilities. We've got to make significant progress before the end of the tournament when folks go home and forget everything. Right now, I'm not making much progress. We have a picture based on input from two unreliable witnesses."

"In other words, status is normal," chirped Karen.

"I guess you're right," sighed Art.

Karen wondered if there was anything else she could do to help move the case along. "Have you totally ruled out a female perpetrator?" she asked.

Art sat up sharply at this question. "No. Not at all. It's just—"

"I know. It's just that men don't think that women are capable of anything."

"Females are capable of many things, but I wouldn't place them high on a record of talented armed robbers. All of the witnesses so far talk about a man."

"Think it through. The weapon used was light and required a little skill. Not a lot. Not hours on a range. It didn't need a mule to lug it around. Lighting fires, setting off fireworks, carrying a bag of money—those are all tasks a woman can do as well as any man."

"Except that a female with a bag of money usually only gets as far as the next clothing store."

"And a man would stop at the first bar. Think about it. Any reasonably fit female could have carried that off easily."

"Okay. I concede. But what about the witnesses? Papan gave us a description of the person she saw in the washroom. She said it was a man."

"Papan told you what she needed to get her forty bucks. You should go back to her and quiz her about the individual she saw. Focus on the physical characteristics."

"Papan's?"

Karen picked up a vase and made a motion to throw it. Art countered with a playful duck. "She got sixty bucks out of me, not forty. But what you say makes sense. I'll talk to her again."

Marge Albas set down the phone after talking to Karen Fraser and held her head in both hands. Karen had explained the investigation of the death of a bridge league official, asking about the possibility of tracing the sale of weapons. When she heard the details of the affair, Marge suspected that a blowgun was involved. She wanted very much to help Karen, and immediately offered to do what she could. As soon as the phone was down, she remembered that she was booked for seminars for the next two days that required out-of-town travel. She had to be back Wednesday night to meet other commitments. *Oh well,* she thought, *I'll have to download the whole file onto my laptop. It's a pretty small file, so that should work. I'll find an opportunity to work on it.*

Ughdart Inc. sold dart weapons that were used to immobilize animals for many reasons. Zoo attendants, veterinarians, and game wardens, among others, found the products invaluable. Fourteen years of service at Ughdart had given her time to understand the product line of rifles, pistols and blow darts along with the variety of projectiles used by each, and to establish a strong rapport with customers. In fact, many folks thought she was the whole order department of the company. She handled new orders, fielded complaints, and directed them, when she couldn't pacify the caller, to technical experts. There were very few that she could not pacify. Her only problem was her boss, Dave.

Dave was a rules person. He believed rules existed for good reasons, and they were to be followed without exception. He was much better at formulating rules than handling customers or dealing with product problems. The sole justification for his position of absolute authority in the company's order processing department was twenty years of service with Ughdart. Marge did her best to get along with Dave. She found that it helped to stay as far away from him as possible, and to avoid talking to him unless it was absolutely necessary.

Part of her job consisted of helping Ughdart sales staff with training seminars that the company offered to their customers. The largest of these groups would be veterinarian students from a university faculty. Ughdart liked to get a whole class to come to their seminars for a half-day session on the use of darts to immobilize large animals. What better way to introduce folks to their product line and generate goodwill among a group who would become lifelong customers?

Marge was plump in a way that made her attractive. Her clothes were tasteful, as a business woman's ought to be—always in style, never stressing any part of her body excessively. She had never had enough self-confidence to enter into a serious relationship with a man. The gratifying feedback she received from participants in the training sessions was a highlight of her life. She was the expert. She was proficient in the use of all of the various Ughdart models. Her classes learned how to subdue an anxious bull that needed medical attention. Marge explained that, unless a person had toreador training, it was wise to keep a safe distance from such an animal, and a rifle model was the best choice. On the other hand, the air pistol format was ideal for immobilizing smaller animals like cats and dogs. Her lectures were followed by actual demonstrations of the use of the products. Salesmen liked her immediately and found her an invaluable resource in generating sales. Students devoted their full attention to her demonstrations and explanations. They had dozens of questions for Marge, and she answered them all with flair and good humor. She never missed these seminars unless she was in the midst of dealing with a critical problem.

Dave happened to walk by her desk within minutes of Karen's call.

"Thinking hard?" he asked.

"Oh my. There's been an accident in Boston involving a dart. An official was killed during a robbery and they've got a big investigation going on."

"What's that got to do with us?" asked Dave.

"They recovered the darts and our logo was on them. Two men were downed and one of them died. The lady who called works for a private detective who's investigating the death."

"You have plenty to do without getting involved with private investigators. If there truly was a death and it's truly important, we'll hear from the Boston police."

Damn, thought Marge. *I knew I shouldn't have started talking to him. I promised the lady I'd help her, and now I'm going to have him on my back.* Dave's attitude put her off the scent, and in the hustle of regular work and preparation for the afternoon training session, she forgot about Karen's call.

Her schedule that afternoon consisted of a seminar involving local folks and a few out-of-towners who were small customers. When she finished, Marge went back to her office to check calls and e-mails. She remembered the request Karen had made and decided to do something about it before she went home. A check of records of blowgun sales over the past three months confirmed her feeling that there had been only a few orders. Most had been sold to zoos and private veterinarian practices, but also a dozen sold to private individuals. She could easily generate the names of customers who had bought the merchandise. She went through the process of downloading the complete file, and left herself a note to clean up the data and organize it in a form that Karen could easily make use of. She would have to find the time to send it to Karen before flying home.

Art sat in the suite, staring vacantly at a landscape painting on the wall, drinking hotel coffee that he could not help comparing to his own special brew. *About half as good*, he thought. *If that.* He mentally reconstructed the investigation, piecing together facts and theories. The killer had to be totally knowledgeable about the work going on at the tournament, the game schedules, the handling of money, the way the hotel organized the work of their staff, and a dozen other matters. He had to know all about the timing of the events, the selling of entries, the short hiatus after entries were closed until the game began, and the approximate dollar value of the entries. The precise timing of the events of the crime convinced Art that the perpetrator had to be a person intimately familiar with the workings of tournament bridge. He could hardly be a complete outsider. He also had to be someone who needed money. That didn't narrow it down much. A hundred and fifty thousand people knew about tournaments, schedules, and hotels. A sizeable portion of the membership had been involved with evacuation drills, which were a matter of policy in various hotels across the country. They all understood how money was handled. Regular attendees at national tournaments would have the know-how to execute a crime like this one, but very few had motive. Only a warped mind would have the ability to work out details and then execute a complete plan. It would take a lot of guts.

A tournament director would qualify as a suspect on several counts, but they were paid a decent salary and most of them liked their work. They were a most unlikely group to produce a criminal who would stage a large robbery with a risk of a fatality. The directors he knew had many shortcomings, but they were generally people of high integrity. His thoughts began to turn more towards a player as a logical suspect. As a group, players comprised such a wide spectrum of humanity that he felt anything was possible. He could think of brilliant people, business leaders, social misfits, billionaires, bums, and everything in between. The more he thought about it, the stronger the notion grew that the perpetrator was a player.

If it were a player, it had to be someone not playing in the Life Master pairs event. In fact, the person could not have been playing in any side games either, morning or afternoon. Preparing for and executing the crime would take all of a person's time and energy that day. So the lists of player entries for the various events of the day would exclude a whole lot of bridge players. The lists were all in computers and could be compiled fairly easily. At least he could start with a smaller list of suspects. He chuckled inwardly at this conclusion. Right now, he had a list with zero names.

He had to get the league to lend him the services of a computer whiz to look at player lists from this year's entries and other years. By comparing the lists, some names would surely pop out. Most directors were good at computers, so the request should be easy to accommodate. With a growing tally of items he needed to do, he was not in for small talk, and to avoid the annoyance of dodging people wandering around the hotel, he found it preferable to use the phone as much as possible. He was about to call the head director when the phone rang. Alan Gilead was on the line.

"Congratulations," said Alan.

Art gave him a puzzled response. "Pardon my ignorance."

"You've pulled in a suspect already. I call that fast work."

"I don't follow."

"Your detective friends pulled in Phil Michaels this morning."

"My what?" said Art. "Pulled in Phil? What in hell for?"

"Weren't you in on the deal?"

"Absolutely not. Tell me who my friends were."

"Julia, the homicide detective, was one. The other was an older guy. The press was here. Photographer as well."

"The older guy would be Bruce Lente. He's in charge of homicide in this district. Somebody made a complete mistake."

"You'd better tell somebody that."

"I guess I'd better. Right now," said Art.

Art thanked him and set his phone down. He explained to Karen what he had just heard.

"You're not the man in charge now, you know," she said.

"I don't know what they're smoking. This is all phony grandstanding."

"That may all be true. Put it in perspective. You're a private investigator. You're a novice at it—this is your first case. You're an unknown as far as the Boston police are concerned. They have no reason to trust you or collaborate with you. The only card you have is goodwill with them. If you don't establish goodwill, you're worse than useless. They won't want to see you around."

"But I can't let Lente bulldoze me into doing things his way. The guy should be out pounding a beat, not running a homicide squad. He's incompetent."

"Fussy, fussy. There's not a thing you can do about it," continued Karen. "You're an outsider here. Lente and his people know nothing about you and care less."

Art digested this little sermon for several moments. "The realities of life. You're right. I'd better make a trip to headquarters and talk to Julia and her captain. This is a grave mistake and a time waster."

"Just how do you plan to convince them that they're full of baloney? I know you'd prefer to shoot straight from the hip, but you ought to try a little harder."

"There are some obvious differences in the composite and the actual photo of Phil. The nose, for instance."

"Okay. That sounds good. Anything else?"

"If anyone saw Phil leaving with the herd when the evacuation order was given, that would clinch it. I need to talk to Fred Jardeen again. About both subjects—Phil and compiling names of possible suspects."

"Now you're cooking. If you go in with something rock solid, they'll have no case. No reason to hold Phil."

He called Fred Jardeen, the head director, to ask for an immediate meeting, explaining the situation regarding Phil Michaels being taken to police headquarters.

"What do you need from me?" asked Fred.

"Boston homicide has pulled Phil Michaels in. I don't know any details and I'm not sure what they're doing with Phil down there. I'm pretty sure they're going totally in the wrong direction."

"What do you want to do about it?"

"Somebody must have seen Phil on Friday, when everything hit the fan and the evacuation order was given. Maybe you did. Picture the scene a few minutes after entries have closed before the game starts. Everything's in limbo. The director in charge makes a few announcements and there are a few directors just talking and waiting for people to be seated and start. Where was Phil? Who was with him?"

"As it happens, I didn't see him. I wasn't paying attention to him anyway. I was trying to figure what was going on. I agree that others must have. He was actually in charge of one of the sections of the championship. He would have been in the main ballroom during the robbery. I'll make a couple of calls and get right back to you."

"Okay," said Art.

When Fred rang back, he said to Art, "Listen. This is hard fact for you. Phil and two other directors made the exit together. Kay and Avery were adamant about Phil's presence."

"Perfect. Thanks. Can I get a short, signed note from each of them? Same note, both signatures?"

"I'll get it to you."

"Right away. I'm going downtown to talk."

Art's spirits rose significantly. He called Boston police headquarters and found that Julia was in, but busy. He left a message that he would be there within a half hour and had something urgent to tell her.

Karen set out a dark blue suit, white shirt, and red-and-blue striped tie.

"You need to look majestic," she said. "Don't go in there looking like a bridge player."

"I thought I was getting rid of bosses," Art chuckled. "Now someone is controlling every move."

"And you love it. While you're mired in your own thoughts, I have a problem."

"Oh. With what?"

"My contact at Ughdart is out of the office for two days, and may not have anything until Friday. I had high hopes."

Art got signed notes from Fred Jardeen about the exact whereabouts of Phil Michaels on Friday at the time of the evacuation. A cab dropped him at police headquarters, and he hurried in to see Bruce Lente. He got through to Lente's office by telling the receptionist that he needed urgently to talk to him. They exchanged greetings, and Lente asked, "Can I hear what you urgently need to tell me?"

"I have some information about Phil Michaels," said Art.

"Will it take long?"

"That depends. I can show you what I've got very quickly. I'm pretty confident you and Julia want to hear me out."

"I can tell Julia. Go ahead."

"I'd rather talk to you both at the same time," insisted Art.

Lente gave him a troubled look, then said, "All right. I'll get Julia. She can use a break now, I'm sure." He instructed his secretary to bring Julia to his office.

Julia appeared at that moment looking more than a little disheveled. Her hair was more tousled than usual and her face showed signs of weariness. "Hi Bruce. You wanted me?" She noticed Art and shook hands.

"Art thinks he's got something we need to see. I thought you'd like a break."

Art took out the photo of Phil Michaels and the final version of the composite the artist had prepared. He explained the differences in features that were clearly evident. "I have two witnesses who swear they were with Phil during the evacuation process. I brought along signed statements from both." Art laid out two letters beside the pictures.

Julia blushed and turned away. Bruce frowned and looked puzzled momentarily, but he hadn't held onto his position for many years by making minor apologies and gratuitous confessions.

"Good information. Very good. Art was with homicide in Buffalo, you know," he said, glancing at Julia, who did know. "How was the homicide group in Buffalo? You had the odd case to handle if I'm right."

"You certainly are right. Some years we have more murders than you do and we're half your size."

"I like the way you say we," chuckled Lente. "Still in the saddle. This working together is paying off. We can use each other." Julia cocked an eyebrow at her boss.

"I'll be glad to have you take all the credit," said Art. "I only want to look good in the eyes of my client."

"Exactly," said Bruce. "Julia, when you're finished with your man, he'll have an unconditional release, and a vote of thanks from us. We'll have a close look at what you found out from him. We can share that with Art."

Art said, "If you are serious about cooperating, we can help each other in several ways."

"We all need help," said Bruce.

"I'm looking into the supplier of dart propellants that immobilized the two directors. Some folks respond better to official police requests than to private detectives."

"Julia will be glad to help."

Julia bit her lip. Art passed on Ughdart's address and phone number.

"I'm done, then," said Art. "I'll head back to the hotel." He was thankful that the taxi ride back to the Westin the trip was quiet, and the conversation abbreviated to destination and fare.

While Art was out, Karen looked out her hotel window towards the Charles River. Seeing bright sunshine, she decided it was time to get some fresh air. She donned the cozy winter coat that, until this year, had been her first line of defense against Buffalo winters, and bundled Clive in his yet unused snow suit. She knew how much Clive liked to be transported around in his sling carrier. She preferred the ancient device to any of the more modern replacements. Strollers and carriages were awkward to maneuver, and in his sling, Clive seemed to enjoy the feeling of being close to her body and the rhythm of her movements. He usually fell asleep in seconds when he was in his sling.

When she had him properly strapped into his carrier, she ventured out into the bright cold world of downtown Boston. She walked down Huntington Street, loving the cold air, and breathed deeply. Clive's face took on a rosy glow and he showed his appreciation by falling fast asleep instantly. In spite of the cold, the street was full of people and cars. Karen found herself dodging this way and that to ensure that no one was bumping into her or her precious cargo.

She had to find a better source of food than the fare they had been eating. When Art was left to himself, he thought little about food and cared less. Cheese sandwiches and frozen dinners were fine as long as he had a good quality diet ginger ale to wash it down. She had no interest in the first-rate, expensive restaurants in Copley Place. Fine dining with wine had no appeal for her as long as Clive was breast-feeding. She and Art had yet to be subjected to his behavior in a restaurant but she felt that this week, in Boston, was neither the time nor the place to try that experiment. She made a note of a decent-looking fast food outlet right in the Westin called Au Bon Pain. The food looked appetizing and there were lots of salads and soups available. Karen thought, *I'll bet a thousand other people have the same idea at mealtimes.* They had not gone far when a sign saying **Shaw's Supermarket** attracted her attention and she went in. In the warm air of the store, Clive continued his deep sleep. The exertion of wheeling a cart through the shelves plus carrying Clive made her wish she had worn lighter clothing. She was surprised to find that a downtown location offered such a massive selection of food items including fresh fruit and vegetables. This looked like a golden opportunity to introduce some tasty and healthy items into their diet. After estimating carefully how much she could carry, she collected a number of items that she felt would stir Art's interest. A huge selection of wines in an upper section of the store sorely tempted her, but she had decided that until she weaned Clive, alcohol was off her list. She noticed a collection of fine Bourbon, and picked up a bottle of single barrel whiskey, which she knew Art would like. With two bags in each hand and Clive slung around her neck, it took only a few steps before she realized how heavy her load had become, and she returned directly to their suite.

Art picked up two vegetarian submarine sandwiches, which he knew Karen liked, and took them up to their suite. "That was a productive trip," he said.

"Phil's been released. Julia's nose is out of joint over the whole affair. I think she feels dumb about it. She should. And the greasy lieutenant waffled his way through the whole discussion."

"Your Honor, may I suggest that nobody asked for your opinion on the witness? Your goal is to fulfill your contract with Alan. Don't you think you'd better hide your ego and get on with the job?"

"You think I should just ignore the incident involving Phil and press on?"

"Absolutely. It's finished. Remember, the lieutenant probably orchestrated the whole act. He may have been the one who suggested bringing Phil in. And who do you think got the press involved?"

"True. At the very least, he must have authorized it. Come to think of it, the D.A. had to be in on it as well."

"Now we've got it. This wasn't Julia the Lone Ranger operating on her own."

"You're right."

"It's easy to sit back and analyze what someone else is doing. Much harder to make right decisions yourself. Let's forget work for a second. I want to show you something."

She led Art to the refrigerator and displayed the cache of food she had purchased. "That store is terrific," she said. "You wouldn't believe all the goodies they have. And look." She proudly displayed the bottle of whiskey she had selected.

Art was not a heavy drinker, but had developed a taste for good Bourbon. He liked an occasional solid belt or two, always on the rocks, never with mix. "That looks great. Evan Williams single barrel," he said, fingering the tag strung around the neck of the bottle. "Gold medal one year, whatever that means. Thanks."

He sheepishly produced the subs he had picked up. "They're okay," said Karen. "But I'm in charge of food from now on."

"My philosophy professor is taking charge of procurement?" smiled Art.

"You might say that," answered Karen.

Back at Boston police headquarters, Julia picked up the phone and connected with Dave at Ughdart. She introduced herself, stated her purpose in calling, then asked for Marge. "Marge is out. Perhaps I can help. I'm the department manager."

"I understand she agreed to help with a list of individuals who purchased your blowgun product."

"Yours is the first official request we've had. She may or may not have agreed to help someone else."

"Really. I understood that Karen Fraser called earlier this week and had a promise for some information. That could be key in our solving the case."

"Let's start from the beginning. Could you identify yourself?"

"I just did."

"I need some way of ensuring that the information goes to the right party. Can you give me your number and I'll call back?"

Julia sighed and gave Dave the number of the Boston police headquarters along with her extension number. When they reconnected, Dave said, "Thanks for accommodating me. Can't be too careful. I'll be glad to see to your request. Now, today's Tuesday. I should be able to get the information for you by next Monday. How does that sound?"

Absolutely rotten, thought Julia. That's four days later than Karen told me. "If that's the best you can do, maybe you could give me the number of the person in charge there. Perhaps your president. We consider this an urgent matter and need to move the investigation along as quickly as possible."

"I understand. It takes a while to assign someone and have them go through all the files. The president couldn't do it any faster than me." He did not mention that Marge was the only person in the company who knew how to assemble the information and that she was away until Thursday. When Julia sheepishly reported the information to Bruce, he absently thanked her for keeping him in the picture.

Art had received several more phone calls in response to the ad in the Monday Bulletin. Even though he held out little hope that they would be valuable, with the current absence of positive leads to work on, he could not afford to overlook any potential clues. He set up a conference room in preparation for the inflow of people he expected to interview. He arranged the chairs in a conversational grouping so that he would not be positioned like a judge passing a sentence. Then he ordered the usual urn of coffee. With everything ready, the first to appear were two elderly grandmothers from Cleveland. Art welcomed them, offered coffee, explained the task he was carrying out, went over his picture in detail, and got rid of them as quickly as possible. This scene repeated itself several more times over the next hour.

Everyone who appeared was interested in the work Art was doing. They wanted to chat about the case, express opinions, and pass on tips as to who might be involved. Not a one of them really knew anyone who was young enough, old enough, thin enough, fit enough, or possessed hair short enough to qualify as a suspect. As he worked through interviews with the dozen players who had accepted his invitation to drop in, Art developed a sinking feeling that his idea of talking to more players had been a clunker. He pictured himself in a room with a large stone fireplace and an empty vodka glass in his hand. He would throw the empty glass hard into the fireplace. Very satisfying. Then he would look for a scapegoat to scold for this dumb idea. Only there were no scapegoats anymore. He was accountable, he alone.

While his morale was stewing at the lowest point in years, an elderly gentleman entered the room.

"Hi. I'm Jim Grove."

"Come in and have a coffee," sighed Art.

"Thanks. I will. That picture you had in the Bulletin—the guy is a dead ringer for Ted Ruhe," he said. "Ted is from Nebraska. He looks just like that."

"Tell me about him," said Art.

"Five foot eight, nine maybe, sandy hair, keeps it short, wiry, thin, smokes like a chimney."

"Bridge player?"

"Oh yes. A good one. He doesn't come to every tournament, but when he shows up, he wins his share."

"Have you seen him here?"

"Yes. He came in Thursday night. I don't know whether he's played yet. I'm hoping to play with him some this week. I like the regional events, not the national games. They're too tough for us."

"Could you see him involved in a robbery and a killing?"

"I doubt if he'd do a thing like that. My guess is he's as straight an arrow as you'll find anywhere. You know how it is with bridge players. You don't ask your partners if they've been to jail. You just sit at the bridge table, have the odd dinner together, spend a little time working out a bidding system, and if you get along, you continue. Usually, you only get into personal stuff if you know them for a long time."

"Anything else you can tell me about Ruhe?"

"I know he can play and he's an okay guy as a partner. I know he's a veterinarian. That's all. All I'm saying is that he looks like the picture you've made up."

"Is he staying at the tournament hotel?"

"We never do. We're both booked in at a Best Western a mile or so away. I haven't seen him for a couple of days though."

"Are you rooming together?"

Grove winked. "No sir. I have the other half of my bed spoken for."

"Okay. Thanks Jim. I'll call your hotel and get in touch with him. If you see him, would you ask him to get in touch with me?"

"Sure."

A call to the Best Western revealed that a Ted Ruhe had checked in the previous Thursday but was not currently available. Art declined to leave a message and decided to visit the hotel personally. While he waited for a cab, he felt the force of Boston winds. The light cotton jacket that he'd brought along from Florida offered little protection. Art chided himself for not bringing the cozy parka he used for Buffalo winters. The cab driver muttered and cursed at the Boston traffic, and by the time they got to the Best Western, Art felt he could have walked there faster. He approached the desk clerk and asked to be shown to the manager's office.

After introducing himself and explaining his involvement in the murder investigation, Art said, "I'd like to ask for your help. I need to talk to one of your guests." Art showed him a picture from the Bulletin.

"Is the gentleman a suspect in the case? Maybe you ought to get the Boston police involved and have the man arrested. I can't have my employees exposed to a big risk."

"I understand your concern. I'm working closely with the Boston police. The person is only wanted for questioning—he's not a suspect, not yet, anyway. We have very little information on this person right now. In all likelihood, he's harmless. There's a slight chance that he's involved, nothing more."

"Okay. So you want us to call you when he shows?"

"That's right. I'll come right over. We should be able to clear the matter up right away."

"Maybe I should phone the Boston police myself and get their opinion."

"That's up to you. I'm working closely with the homicide department. I suggest you wait until I've talked to the man. If I find anything suspicious, I'll be in touch with them immediately. I'm sure you have other things to do and so do they."

"All right then. I'll go along with you. But I can't say I like it."

On the way out of the hotel, Art took a deep breath of the cold fresh air, noted the bright sunshine, and decided to walk back to the Westin. He would skip the cab ride. Reaching Massachusetts Avenue took less than a minute, plenty of time for the cold to penetrate his thin clothing and make him question whether he had made a bad decision. It seemed as though someone had turned down the thermostat on the downtown area. The skyscrapers blocked the sun and served as channels for the winds. He felt heat draining from his body. His ears started to tingle as the cold air drained heat, and covering them with icy hands brought little relief. He increased his pace a few notches, turned his flimsy collar up, and stuffed his hands in his pockets. When he reached Huntington Street, he was feeling almost comfortable. By the time he entered the Westin, the effort had left him with a feeling of exhilaration. As he walked, he had a suspicion that Mr. Best Western was going to call Boston police headquarters anyway, and that he could expect to hear from Julia about keeping her informed

Back in the suite, he shared a quick sandwich with Karen. She had some news. "Mary McGee phoned. She says she knows someone who resembles the picture."

"Who's Mary? We ought to get her up here."

"I asked her to come up at twelve-thirty. She's a director. Lives in Louisiana. You'd know her if you saw her."

"Maybe. There are so many out there, I can't remember them all. And they don't identify themselves well."

"She said something about a caddy. I couldn't pick up her meaning."

"It can't hurt to talk to her. Any lead is welcome."

Mary turned up as promised. Art recognized her as a director with whom he'd had a run-in a few years earlier. He had disagreed on a ruling she'd made and insisted on a committee to review the matter. According to the bylaws of the bridge league, Mary was required to convene a small group to review the protest and see to the presentation of all of the facts. Part of her job was to address the committee and provide details of the bridge laws governing the situation. Mary had appointed three prominent bridge players to serve as a jury. The hearing had operated in the manner of a small-scale trial, with Art as the prosecution and his opponents as the defense. All of this extra effort plus the delay in getting a score on the hand under protest had resulted in a delay in posting the results of the event. The committee upheld Art's protest and overturned her initial ruling, and Mary had been cool ever since. He wondered if she remembered the incident. His question was quickly answered.

"If it isn't Mr. Committee himself. How are you?"

"You have a good memory," said Art. "That was a day or two ago."

"Four years, actually," said Mary. "No hard feelings. It's all part of a day's work. Look, I thought I should get in touch. I saw the picture you plastered on the Bulletin and it's a dead ringer for one of the caddies."

"Caddy?" echoed both Karen and Art.

"Yes. I swear it's the same person. You know, in some places the caddies are all kids. Relatives of the players, often relatives of the board members. But not always. There are places where older people are looking for work, and they're glad to get the minimum wage we offer. Most of them are unemployed and know nothing about the game. Then there's this group of kids who travel all over North America on caddy work. One of them has an old jalopy and he provides a bus service for the rest. They go all over the U.S. But the person I'm speaking of is older. He must be in his early thirties."

"That's very interesting," said Karen.

"In any case, that's my scoop for the day," added Mary.

"Thanks, Mary," said Art. "What's the best way to get in touch with this person? Do you know his name?"

"Sorry, no name for you. But check with Dot Jefe. She's the caddy master, and she's staying here at the Westin."

"Maybe she's available right now. Can you come with me?"

"Sure."

When Art called Dot's number, he got a voicemail message saying that she was out and would be back the next day. "Damn," said Art. "Can't talk to her until tomorrow."

"I think she has relatives here in Boston," said Mary. "She may be back later tonight. Why don't you leave a message anyway?"

Art thought this was a good idea, and hoped that they might be able to talk to the caddy that evening.

Mary said, "I've got to go now. If I see the caddy around this afternoon, I'll get in touch right away." Later that afternoon, she called and remembered that the caddy's name was Bobby Rideau. Nobody had seen him that day.

Shortly after Mary left, Art got a call from the manager at the Best Western. "Your party just checked out."

"Is he still around?"

"He took a cab to the airport right after he paid his bill."

Art said, "Do you have an address or phone number so I can contact him?"

"I can't do that without an official police warrant. I can't just go on the word of a private investigator."

"All right. I'll be in touch," said Art and hung up. He thought, *I'll have to get in touch with Julia to make the request official. I could have handled the situation differently. Contacted Julia in the first place. Had the room searched. Had someone watch the room until Ruhe returned. Ruhe must have come back to pack. Someone must have seen him. I'll need a lot more cooperation if the case is going to end quickly and successfully. I had a lot more clout when I was a regular homicide detective. Did Jim know that Ruhe was taking off?*

He decided to contact Jim Grove when the afternoon session was finished and get the home phone number of Ruhe. That would bypass all of the bureaucratic red tape he'd face if he involved Julia. He went up to the convention floor just before five and found the room where Jim was playing. He knew he would be dodging questions from everyone who knew him, and his circle of acquaintances had grown steadily all week. He kept a smile on his face the whole time, remembering a note he had read recently that it is easier to fake happiness than any other emotion. He was faking it all right.

He dragged Jim away from his partner and sat down with him at a deserted table. "Any idea where Ruhe could be?"

"Well, if he's not at the Best Western, I have no idea."

"He checked out at noon today," said Art.

"Hell. I was hoping we could play tomorrow. I wonder what's going on."

"Have you got his phone number, address, or any way to contact him?"

"Sure. Back on my computer in Oklahoma."

"Is there any way we could get it?"

"I'm a widower. There's no one at my place right now. Try the white pages on the internet. There can't be a whole lot of Ruhes in Omaha."

"I guess that's the best I can do." Art stopped himself from expressing the frustration that he was feeling. Delays were everywhere. Except for Karen, nobody showed a sense of urgency about the investigation. Every imaginable sidetrack seemed to surface and prolong the time it took to pin down a single piece of useful information. "I was hoping to keep things moving. If we don't make progress on this thing before the tournament is over, we may have to forget about solving it."

"Listen," said Jim. "The ACBL has information on all our members and their addresses. Try one of the directors."

"Thanks," said Art, deciding to skip the details on how much effort he had already invested in doing just that.

He called the Boston Police station, hoping to catch Julia before she left for the day. His luck was in. "I have another lead that needs to be checked out," said Art. "This one will need your help."

"Tell me," answered Julia.

"We got this one from the picture your artist produced. A guy by the name of Ted Ruhe, who lives in Omaha, is evidently a pretty good match for the picture. The face and the build are very close to the description we published. From what I know, he got here last Thursday and left in a hurry today. We haven't been able to contact him."

"Do you have the usual wealth of background details? I suppose he's another of your players whose only known character trait is his bridge skill."

Art was about to make an impulsive response to this, then realized that Julia's assessment was right. "That's ironic, but true. We can play bridge with someone for years and never know if a partner's source of income is robbing banks or clipping coupons. I'm afraid I know very little about Ruhe. The only facts we have on him are that he's a regular bridge player and a veterinarian in real life. Most vets have a good working knowledge of blowguns and darts. If he does, he qualifies as a prime suspect."

"This could get interesting. He lives in Nebraska? Do you have his home address and phone?"

"I don't think I have the right number for him. I tried a couple of numbers for Ruhe in Omaha. I did manage to contact a lady who says that she's Ruhe's ex-wife, that he's a cheater and owes her child support payments. She asked if I knew where he was and how to get in touch with him."

"Sounds like a real winner," said Julia.

"Truly. But she admitted that her husband wasn't a veterinarian. I really don't think using public facilities to track him down is the answer. You and Bruce would have more clout getting information across state boundaries than I would. This may just be a case of his not being home. He was expected to play here later this week. We have no other personal information, no family background."

"Okay. Pass it on and I'll get busy with it," said Julia, showing more enthusiasm than she had in all their previous discussions. "I can push through some data on Ruhe on our internet loop. Bruce would be the best person to make an official contact with the Omaha police."

"Ruhe was staying at the Best Western a few blocks over. I just missed him when I went to check on him yesterday. They wouldn't give out any personal information without a warrant. You could find a trail of his activities from his credit card and other info."

"Thanks for letting me in on the scoop early," said Julia. "Okay. I'll pick that up and pay them a visit. If the Best Western needs a warrant for a simple matter like that, they may find they have difficulties getting police help when they need it."

As they hung up, Julia indicated that she would be in touch shortly. Art was about to apologize and make an excuse for not contacting her sooner to get a warrant, then decided that their relationship was moving in a positive direction. The tension between the two of them had been fading. Pursuing the issue further would risk reopening a wound that was healing over.

Julia dropped in to Lente's office and reported on her skimpy progress. "There's a guy in Nebraska who may come close to being a suspect. He matches the composite picture and was here during the time of the crime. It seems that he suddenly decided to take off for Omaha."

"Sounds sketchy," answered Bruce. "Did you find out anything else about him?"

"We do know that he's a veterinarian. That means he'd likely be familiar with the use of these immobilization darts that killed the victim."

"Well now. That makes it interesting. This sounds like a man we should get to know. Maybe somebody ought to travel to Omaha and talk to him."

"All we picked up on a phone call was a talk to an ex-wife who says he's behind in child support payments."

"How is it that we can talk to the ex-wife, but not to Mr. Ruhe himself?"

"We must have had the wrong Ruhe. The ex-wife says her husband wasn't a veterinarian. I assume that the right Ruhe is en route right now, and we'll be able to track him down when he lands and settles down in Omaha. Getting through to the woman was a fluke. Fraser got her number somehow and put in a speculative call. Think you could contact somebody out there?"

"Omaha? Sure. I have an old friend there, John Marshall. I'll call him right now. He'll be able to find out about the Ruhe family and their whereabouts. Give me half an hour. If I get lucky, I'll connect right away and get everything started pronto."

"Ruhe stayed at the Best Western downtown. I'm going to get his credit card and other info from them. I'll put a trace on him when I get some document numbers. Be back in thirty minutes," said Julia.

John Marshall was at his desk in Omaha police headquarters when Bruce Lente phoned. Now a captain in the Omaha city police, Marshall and Lente had been close buddies in the marines thirty years ago. Their mutual trust and respect had remained strong over the three decades since. "John, we got a robbery and murder here in Boston and a suspect from Omaha. I could use a little help."

"What makes you think anyone in Omaha would help an easterner?" asked John.

"I don't know yet, but I'm going to push my luck a bit. The guy's name is Ruhe. All we know is he's a veterinarian from Omaha and divorced. I'd like a little background on him and his family. He was in Boston at the time of the murder and fits a number of scenarios that make us suspicious. He picked up and left town all of a sudden before we could talk to him."

"Could your department afford a plane ride to Omaha? Come on down for a visit. We could look up Ruhe together and get your answers."

"That seems like a lot of trouble for a few simple answers," said Lente.

"Come on. How's your budget running? Expenses twenty percent under plan as usual?"

"That's never happened. Maybe you get away with phony budgets, but our guys are too sharp to let that through."

"We have big steaks out here. We could knock back a couple of beers while we're at it. We haven't done that for a long time."

"You're making it sound pretty important. I'd better take a close look."

"Perfect. Confirm your intentions when you figure them out."

"Naturally."

CHAPTER 7

KAREN AND CLIVE WERE STILL SLEEPING when Art awoke. He dressed and silently exempted himself from his usual morning duties. Slipping out of the suite, he headed for Starbucks. Their coffee and muffins had been on his list for a trial. He judged the coffee fair, almost equal to his own, and the muffin very good. While munching and sipping, he phoned Chris to ask him to send Papan down to the conference room that he was using. She showed up looking lovely, as only Papan could, with her jet-black hair neatly done and a perfect shade of lipstick complementing her colors. She offered a shy smile and took the chair that Art proffered.

"Busy?" asked Art.

"Not so bad today. Plenty of people moved out. I got lots to do though."

"Take a look at this picture." Art pulled out the composite drawing that Joe Karsh had prepared.

"Yes. He's the one," said Papan.

"Now, how tall would you say he was?"

"Taller than me, for sure."

"How much taller?"

"Ooh. Hard to say. He was across the room when I mopped the floor."

Art began to wonder how much of the person Papan really saw. "Did he stand up straight?"

"Oh yes. Let me see. Straight? Yes. About up to the top of the towels. Where the towels come out. The holder for the towels. The top of that."

"Okay. Is that higher than you?"

"Me? Oh yes," Papan laughed. "I only come up to here." She gestured a few inches above her head.

"So the person was maybe six inches taller than you?"

"Yes, I think so. Maybe six inches."

Art was not sure whether he was making progress or not. Papan seemed to agree with his last words every time he spoke.

"Maybe a foot taller?"

"On no, Mr. Fraser. Not a foot. Definitely six inches."

That sounded better. "And he was fatter than you?"

She laughed again. "No, no. I am much fatter. I mean the person was skinny. Really skinny."

Art thought, if Papan is much fatter, the person she saw was a toothpick.

"Okay. So we have a tall, thin person. Was the person a woman?"

This startled Papan. "A woman?" She laughed. "No, Mr. Fraser. He was not a woman. I know a man and a woman."

"How did you know?"

"Look at the hair. You ever see a woman with hair short like that? I like long hair. Women like long hair."

"Was there anything else that makes you think it was a man?" Art made a gesture implying fullness of bosom. Papan laughed again."

"You mean tits? He had no tits, Mr. Fraser. Not like me." She thought this was hilarious.

"How about a tall, thin woman with no tits, and her hair cut short?"

Papan stopped laughing. She did not know what to say. "Okay. You don't believe me. I can't help that."

"Papan, I do believe you. But it is very important to make sure the person you saw is either definitely a man or a woman. Did the person speak at all?"

"No. Said nothing."

"Did he carry anything heavy?"

"No. Yes. I mean was carrying nothing heavy. A little bag. I didn't see."

"Then maybe it could have been a woman?"

Papan was totally serious now, deep in thought. "I think possibly it could have been a woman. But a very strange woman. He had all this short hair. No woman has short hair."

"What color was his hair?"

"I told Joe it's brown. Just like he put in the picture. Light brown. Not blonde. Not nice and black like me."

Art told her he did believe her, thanked her for her help, and sent her back to her job. *Karen is right*, he thought. *The perp could definitely be a woman. Maybe not terribly strong, but strong enough and very fit to move around like that. Someone between thirty and forty, probably.*

When he returned to his suite, he found Karen busily attending to Clive. He took over his usual job as morning chef and served breakfast. "I just had a chat with Papan."

"Your regular duty," said Karen.

"Somebody has to. She's not totally convincing on the gender of the perp. He looked and was dressed like a man, but there's room for doubt."

"I won't say I told you so."

Alan Gilead phoned Art with some news. "Some bridge bucks with Friday's serial numbers have shown up. One hundred and forty dollars worth—the price of a regionally rated team entry, less some change."

"Tell me about it."

"We've them set aside. They were used to buy entries to a Swiss team game yesterday. Unfortunately, we didn't get the person who used them. Come on down to the directors' room and I'll get Henry Katz and we'll talk it over. George Piccole directed the Swiss game. I'll get him in as well."

Art went down immediately. Alan and Henry were waiting for him. Alan mentioned that George would be coming shortly. Henry said, "Finding bridge bucks with serial numbers in that range doesn't necessarily mean anything. All it tells us is that these bills were sold on Friday."

"I agree," said Art. "We're looking for a huge coincidence, but let's not rule it out. We're going to get lucky sooner or later. Suppose these bills were part of the haul that our perpetrator walked off with. Then suppose that he decided that the bills were too hot for him to make use of. He abandoned them. Maybe he left them in a room when he checked out. If he threw them in a garbage container, they would have ended up in the garbage and someone found them. If he left them easily visible in the room, same thing. It's also possible that he left them hidden in a room and the cleaning staff didn't notice them. They stayed there, and the next person to rent the room spotted them. One way or another, they were abandoned, then found and then used to buy entries. If we find the person who found them, we have a big lead. Especially if we uncover where he found them."

Alan added, "It's also possible that someone in the cleaning staff found them in a room that had been vacated, where the person checked out and left the bills behind. The housekeeper may have wondered what to do with them. She could have looked for someone to ask and found the wrong person. That person may have relieved her of the responsibility, took the bills off her hands."

George Piccole showed up at this point and listened to the conversation.

Art said, "There are several possibilities here. One thing is for sure. If the guy who found the bucks used them once, he'll use them again. Let's not second guess ourselves. We need some hard facts. Let's focus on being on the lookout to see if this series is used again in the next couple of days. Can we narrow our search down any? For instance, George, have you an idea when the bills were used?"

"No, I don't. Unfortunately, I only spotted the numbers when I was reconciling the total take for the event. You know, I recounted all the money, the checks, and the bridge bucks and entered the data in an official accounting memo."

Alan said, "Remember we found exactly one hundred and forty dollars worth of bridge bucks in the right range of serial numbers. The cost of an entry for a team is sixty-two dollars a session. The bridge bucks only come in multiples of twenty dollars, so a hundred and forty bucks would buy an entry for a two-session team game—afternoon and evening. That amount of money pins it down exactly to a two-session Swiss team event, not a knockout and not a pairs contest."

"Good point," agreed Art. "A two-session regionally rated Swiss team game. Alan, I think we had better distribute another note to all of the directors selling entries. Maybe you can double up on the staff at the selling desks. Check all of the bridge bucks coming in and keep a record of who's using them."

Alan sat quietly for a moment. "That's not asking much," he said. Art was about to reinforce his request when Alan continued. "We'll do what we can. I know that every lead is potentially important. I'll talk to Fred Jardeen and we'll get a note out right away."

George said, "Maybe we only need to keep watch on the side games. We're agreeing that the money we recovered so far came from a Swiss team game. That means that your suspect is not playing in any of the championship events. Plus, you can be pretty sure that the guy isn't a well-known player. Somebody would have spotted him by now."

"That'll cut down some on extra work," conceded Art. "You may be right. Okay. Let's try it. We'll do that and touch base right after the entry fees are counted for each session."

Alan agreed and the meeting broke up.

~  ~

Alan Gilead called Art at two that afternoon, after the entry fees for the afternoon had been tallied and properly accounted for. "We got some more bridge bucks, Art."

"No kidding. Any luck identifying the person using them?"

"You bet. We doubled up our staff selling entries at the side games. When the bucks came in, we set them aside. We got a guy buying a knockout team entry and the serial numbers on the bucks he used were a match. In fact, they followed right after the bills we took in yesterday. Eighty dollars this time."

"I'll come right down. Can we get Henry Katz again?"

Alan chuckled. "I thought you'd ask that. Yes, we can. I told Fred to spring him from the game he's working on."

Art arrived at the same time as Henry and they joined Alan at a small conference table. "What do we know about the guy passing the dollars?" asked Art.

Henry spoke up. "First of all, this could be entirely legitimate. He could have bought a bunch on Friday and have plans to use them all week."

"True," said Art. "Have you got records of the purchases made on Friday?"

"I do," said Henry. "We have an archaic old machine with a telephone modem on it. It gets all the authorizations for the purchases and stores all of the records in our computer."

"Let's take a look at those records," said Alan. "Who bought this entry?"

"Steve Richards. He's from Florida," said Fred.

"Was he in the game yesterday where the bucks were used with suspicious serial numbers?" asked Art.

"I have no idea," said Henry.

"We'll soon find out," said Alan. "I'll get hold of George. He can look it up easily."

Wednesday was the final day of Marge Albas' trip to the University of California School of Veterinary Medicine in Davis, California. She was about to participate in a three-hour seminar on the use of Ughdart products. Even though she was totally familiar with the routine she was about to direct and had done it many times, she looked forward to the day. She liked young people, and had a repertoire of good jokes to spice up her presentation. The salesman responsible for the territory, Brian Black, had given his usual humorous introduction and put the group of eighteen students in a good frame of mind. The session went well, as Marge knew it would. Her marksmanship with rifle, pistol, and blowgun was outstanding, and the class was suitably impressed.

When she finished the session, she and Brian had lunch, and she found she had a couple of hours before catching a taxi to the airport. She went to a spot in the university library where she could set up her laptop, tie in to a wireless network, and dig into the Ughdart database containing information on all commercial transactions.

The wireless internet connection at the university was user-friendly. She connected easily to the corporate website, and was able to gain access to all of Ughdart's sales data, and then to extract details of blowgun sales for the past twelve months. She chose to itemize both commercial and private sales, then split the data into two sections. She decided to pass both on to Karen, made up a clearly marked file, and attached it to an e-mail. When she'd finished, she found that she had only a little time to spare to make her flight. She put her machine away and headed for the airport.

Art and Karen were alone in their sitting room, with Clive asleep in the bedroom. Art said, "We have a tiny lead involving bridge bucks. We've had two incidences where someone has used bridge bucks that were sold prior to the Life Masters' Pairs on Friday. They were probably used during that event and retrieved by somebody, somewhere. We're trying to track that down now."

"I don't understand."

"If, and this is a big if, the robber dumped the bridge bucks he acquired during the robbery, and someone came across them and started using them, we'd like to know how it all happened. Not to mention where and when."

"Couldn't somebody have bought a wad of bucks Friday and just got around to using them now?"

"Absolutely. That's why I say a big if. On the other hand, maybe the person using them didn't buy them. Acquired them illegally. That's what we're checking."

"Good luck."

When Karen turned on her computer, she was excited to find a note flashing on her e-mail. When she saw it was from Marge, she could hardly wait to read it.

> Hi Karen
>
> I have attached two spreadsheets showing lists of buyers of blowguns for you. One list covers the past six months. The other goes back twelve months. If you need more than that, please get in touch.
>
> Best regards,
>
> Marge

Karen was thrilled with the news. She began to think about how to make use of the data. She printed off the two lists and looked at the short one first. "Hey, Art," she called. "Take a look."

Art came over and sat beside her. He went down the shorter list with Karen. He saw no familiar names. "No help there. At least not yet," said Art.

"No. Here's the other one."

"The twelve month list is probably the one we want."

Karen asked, "Why do you say that?"

"The whole robbery scheme was well planned," responded Art. "It probably took our perpetrator a long time to work out. He may have ordered his materials well in advance of the actual robbery. That's why I think it's more likely we will find the person's name on the longer list. It only has about a hundred names anyway. That shouldn't be too hard to deal with."

"There's a T. Ruhe from Omaha," Karen pointed out.

"That must be the guy we're looking for," agreed Art. "We know Ruhe is a veterinarian, so it's not surprising that his name is here."

"Ruhe certainly sounds like a promising lead."

"I'd better let Julia know that he was a recent Ughdart customer. Tracing him should have priority at this point." When he called Julia, she expressed interest in the finding and agreed with Art about priority.

They continued looking carefully over the list and spotted a few other names that seemed familiar, but there was nothing conclusive. "I need to discuss this with someone who knows the database and see what he wants to do. He'll probably want an electronic copy so that he can work on it without having to keyboard all the names in."

"That's no problem," said Karen.

"I'm hoping someone can compare this list with the ACBL membership and see what pops up. Apart from Ruhe, some of these buyers must be ACBL members."

"You're going to do some list work."

"Right now I'm listless. I'm thinking that if I could get my hands on a shortlist of suspects, we'd be able to use that to get a useful lead. Getting a meaningful shortlist is the hurdle. Our perpetrator has to be someone who was around the playing area but not playing."

Karen said, "Your suspect may not have been a player at all."

"It had to be either a player or a director. I'm leaning more towards a player."

"Okay. Theoretically, you can't rule out others. But you have to start somewhere to narrow down possibilities. How will you get your names?"

"The people who were playing are all recorded in the director's computers. That part is easy. The people who were around but not playing are a problem. I'm not sure how to do that."

Karen replied, "If you start with all of the ACBL members, you'll have a whopping list of names."

"True," said Art. "But maybe a light will go on when we start playing with the data."

"What about the registration desk? Do they enter names into a computer, or just make up the lists by hand?"

Art answered, "I'm pretty sure it's all manual. People show up and sign their name on a file card, along with the place where they're staying. Volunteers, not professional staff, look after the files. Their data isn't complete either, since there's no requirement for anyone to register. Some people like the bag of goodies the registration people hand out. If a person doesn't care about those things, he won't bother registering. When you think about it, anyone planning to stage a robbery would be a fool to register. We ought to be treating the registration list as a group who had nothing to do with the robbery and killing."

"That's an interesting point. I think you're right."

"I've already been down to talk to the volunteers there. I should have thought of this before. Anyway, I've got to hope that I can somehow produce a shortlist, something we'll be able to handle. Then I'll have to go through it and make judgments about who we class as a suspect."

"Sounds like a lot of work," said Karen. "The worst part is that there's no guarantee it'll produce anything useful."

"That's par for homicide investigations. Every lead is a potential blind alley. Anyway, your data from the dart company is a solid place to start."

Art phoned Fred Jardeen. "Fred, I have another one for you. I'd like to do some work with one of your guys who's totally familiar with the ACBL databases. You know, membership lists and so on. I'm becoming convinced that the culprit was a player, and someone not playing at all in this tournament. Then the dart company has given us a list of people who've bought those immobilization darts and blowguns over the past twelve months. I'd like to check that against the ACBL membership list. Other ideas may crop up if I get talking to someone who can get at the information."

Fred gave him the name of someone he would assign. "Jeff Gatling will love that. He sleeps with his computer, and he has access to all kinds of files: national tournament files; headquarters files; almost anything you can name. You can work here in the director's office if you like. Have you met Jeff?"

"I don't think so. Can't recall, anyway."

"Machine Gun Gatling, we call him. He talks like a machine gun, in bursts, not sentences. Grammar is a mystery to him."

"I definitely haven't had the pleasure."

"Your best bet in talking to him is to start by asking advice. He hates to take specific instructions from anyone. If you give him some rope, he may surprise you."

"I understand," responded Art.

"I'll get him to call you."

Jeff Gatling phoned shortly after. Art indicated that he wanted to dig into some membership data and explore whether he could turn up some leads on his investigation. He asked Jeff about the best time to get together. He thought that Jeff sounded like a sprinter in the blocks. "C'mon right down. Now. Got a complete membership list on my machine. Run a compare function when you bring down your dart list. Can download lists of who's playing here. There are other ways of slicing data. Maybe other approaches we can look at."

Art took the e-mail note that Karen had copied onto a memory stick and headed directly for the directors' room. He found Jeff there, engrossed in looking at a screen and muttering to himself.

"How's it going?" asked Art.

"Shit. Oh, hi Art. Great. Gimme a minute. Just hit the wrong key. There we go. Okay. What we going to do?"

"I'm trying to get a list of suspects I can work through to nail down the guy who pulled off the robbery and killing on Friday. I'm wondering if there's any way we can work together."

"Well, start with a hundred and fifty thousand members in the U.S. and Canada. We can carve that up in several ways. Males only? Cuts the list in half."

Art was about to nod affirmatively until he remembered his conversation with Karen. "We're not one hundred percent sure of the gender. Let's leave that."

"Check. Male and female," continued Jeff. "Let's think about what you need. Names of legitimate suspects. Somebody not playing. Directors you know about. Very short list. You can check them out easily. Now, your picture in the Bulletin. From that, your man has to be a certain age. Twenty to forty. Maybe twenty-five to thirty-five."

Art said, "More like thirty to forty."

"Could tabulate all the players in that age group. Boils it down a lot. But we're still talking thirty or forty thousand."

"I wondered about players who showed up at previous national tournaments but are not playing here. Would that help us? They may be on the scene and not playing."

Jeff clicked away at his machine for a few minutes. "There were seven thousand players in Vegas. Seven thousand four hundred and ten, to be exact. Don't know what in hell we can do with that list. What do you think?"

Art winced. "I have no idea. That's not going to help us. A useful shortlist would have to be under a hundred."

"Any way we can narrow it down further?"

Art sat for a moment, thinking. "Masterpoints?"

"Nope. Even at zero to two masterpoints you have ten thousand players. Place of residence? That would really cut it down."

"Right now we have no idea. It could be anywhere in the U.S., or Canada for that matter. It looks like our only leads will be blowgun and dart purchases. I have a list of names and addresses of about a hundred people who bought supplies in the past twelve months. We could see how many of those are ACBL members."

"Agree. I'll go ahead and set that up. Give you a short list for sure. May not be inclusive though."

"I guess that's the best we can do." Art handed the memory stick to Jeff.

After a few minutes of manipulation, Jeff muttered, "Damn. Wrong format." Correcting this took another few minutes, at which point he was ready to run comparisons. "Here we go." Shortly after that, Jeff passed back the stick, which now had the names of a dozen buyers who were ACBL members. Art took the tiny drive, thanked Jeff and returned to his suite.

Karen looked at the list with him. "I suppose when our man ordered materials from Ughdart, he wouldn't necessarily have had them delivered to his home. Marge's data shows shipping addresses, not residential addresses. It's easy to set up a postal box, or use some dodge to hide an identity."

Art said, "One step at a time. We'll see where we get with what we have right now. I need to find out if any of these names are known to directors."

"We're going to wear the directors out with our questions," said Karen.

"Let's not worry about that. They're committed to helping us. Fred Jardeen and Alan are one hundred percent behind us."

Art called Fred Jardeen and told him about his progress. Fred responded, "You've got a pretty short list. It won't take long to look it over and reach some conclusions. I'm heading for lunch with a couple of other directors. Bring your list and we'll go over it."

"Where do you guys go for lunch?" asked Art.

"We generally go to Au Bon Pain. They run a bakery café—bake stuff on the premises. All the food is fresh. They sell most things by the pound."

"How much for a pound of beer?" asked Art.

"Sorry, no booze. Coffee, tea, and juices. The service is cafeteria style, and if we go a bit early, say quarter to twelve, we miss the big lineups. Plus the selection is better. If you haven't tried it, you'll like it. You can get there from the Westin lobby or from Huntington Street."

Art made a few extra copies of his list of names and headed for Au Bon Pain. He spotted his colleagues, got in the lineup and selected a few items from the buffet. A large helping of Caesar salad made up most of the weight of his food, but he couldn't resist adding some cold salmon and small heaps of radishes and onions. The cashier weighed it all and collected Art's money. He joined Fred and two other directors, passed out copies of his list and started the discussion. They were able to exclude most of the names they saw. After eliminating infirm and incapacitated individuals, as well as those who could not possibly be suspects for reasons of character, Art was left with four names to deal with.

"Go to the registration desk," said Fred. "Those people may have registered there, and you can find out where they're staying."

"As a matter of fact, Karen and I discussed this. We think that anyone who registered should be excluded from the list of suspects. The last thing our perpetrator would do is to advertise the fact that he's on the premises. I'd use the registration folks as a way to exclude suspects."

"Checking the front desk at both the Westin and the Marriott might help," added Fred.

"That sounds worthwhile," said Art. "I'll get Alan to clear me for security. I don't want a hassle when I start asking questions. Thanks guys."

Julia dropped into Lente's office and announced that she had a news item. "We know from Ughdart's records that Ted Ruhe from Omaha is a customer of theirs. He's bought several blowguns over the past two years."

Lente replied, "That is news. I was hoping you'd tell me that." In short order, he was able to put a half-formed plan into motion. He found that he could get a late afternoon plane to Omaha, through Chicago, and booked it along with a reservation at an airport hotel. He then called his buddy, John Marshall, to let him know he would be in his office at eight a.m. the next day.

"Hey, I knew you could do it," said Marshall.

When Julia returned, Lente surprised her by informing her that he was going to Omaha that night. "I may bring Ruhe back with me."

Julia was used to some of Lente's precipitous acts, but she found this one dumbfounding. "Good luck. I didn't know we had enough information to bring him in."

"We don't now, but I may have by the time I finish talking to him. We can't just sit around hoping."

"I agree with that. Who can I talk to while you're gone?" she asked.

"I'll only be away for a day or so. You can handle things for that time, I hope. Anyway, call Bill Steele if you have questions or need backup for anything."

Julia was happy about that.

Art went to Alan's suite to discuss the status of the bridge bucks investigation. Alan reported, "I've got a couple of new items. Richards was definitely playing in the Swiss game yesterday. He probably bought the entry then, as well as today. Henry also looked up the purchase records for the first Friday—for Richards and for his three teammates. He played with the same three people both days—yesterday and today. No one on the team bought bridge bucks on Friday. Of course, Henry also adds a disclaimer—he doesn't guarantee that his records are one hundred percent accurate."

"Henry loves details. It's a good thing he does," commented Art. "So the bucks are almost certainly from the Friday entries. That means they were part of the loot our killer took away. We need to question Richards ASAP. I ought to get Julia Baker in on the deal too. I'll call her and get her over here."

"Can you do it before the game starts?"

"You mean you don't want to see Richards miss his evening session?" Art smiled.

"I was thinking that, yes. Couldn't help it. I suppose in the outside world nobody would bother with such a thing. But if Richards isn't guilty of anything, there's no point in punishing him."

"I'll get Julia right now." Art took out his cell phone, dialed Julia and told her they had a person they wanted to question immediately, and she was needed for the interrogation. She said she would be there as soon as she finished what she was doing. Art asked for a specific time and she quoted six-thirty. Art extracted a promise that she wouldn't be a minute late.

"We need to get Richards here at six forty-five. How do we attract his attention?" asked Art.

"Fred Jardeen can be very persuasive with the players. I'll tell him to lean on Richards," answered Alan. "Who do we want at our meeting? You, me, Julia and Richards. Any directors?"

"We want to find out exactly how Richards came by that particular set of bridge bucks. As a matter of fact, I'm not even sure that you should attend. The questions may get rough. You can only lose by being there. Stories get around. They get warped, too. By the time they get back to you, they might have you committing the murder. Julia and I should handle it."

"Okay. Your call. I'll get in touch with Jardeen and arrange for Richards to get down here. You said six forty-five?"

"Julia says she'll be here at six-thirty. I need a couple of minutes to brief her."

"Richards and his gang will probably be having dinner."

"You said Fred can be persuasive."

Alan sighed. "Alright. I'll get him here at six forty-five."

Julia arrived shortly after her promised time with Bill Steele in tow. They talked to a concierge and came up to the conference room where Art was waiting.

She explained Steele's presence. "Bill's a senior member of the department. He's backing me up while Bruce is out of town."

Art shook hands with Steele. "You're working late."

"That's part of the territory," smiled Steele.

"Things too hot for Bruce?"

Julia responded, "He's planning to arrest a veterinarian from Omaha."

Fraser made a funny face. Steele asked, "Tell us about bridge bucks. I've never heard of them before."

Art explained the process. "The league's had this pseudo currency in circulation for over a decade. Everyone calls the stuff bridge bucks. They're yellow strips of paper the size of regular currency, printed with either twenty or fifty dollar notation. Members buy them from the league using VISA or MasterCard for all the usual marketing reasons – conserve cash and get airmiles or hotel credits They're only useful for purchases from the league—entries to competitions and certain merchandise. A wad of these bills—about four thousand dollars worth—was taken in the robbery and murder on Friday. We're pretty sure the guy we're about to talk to is using bills from that particular lot. I expect he wasn't our perpetrator. I think he came across a wad of these bills illegally. Maybe he found them. Maybe he got them from the hotel cleaning staff. One sure fact is that he's using stolen property to pay his entry fees. It may well be that our perp decided the bridge bucks and the checks were useless and abandoned them somewhere."

Steele asked, "Will this connect with our perpetrator?"

"That's not clear yet. What is clear is that the man we're going to talk to, his name is Richards, possesses stolen property. I doubt he's the killer. In fact, right now, I don't know what we could even charge him with. Laws don't cover bridge bucks. Not yet, anyway."

"I see. But if we can find out how he came across the money, we may get something there to lead us to our perp," Steele said.

"Exactly."

Their conversation was interrupted by a knock. Fred Jardeen walked in with a middle-aged, balding man. "Meet Steve Richards," said Fred.

Art thanked Fred, who left quickly. Art shook hands and introduced Julia and Bill as detectives from the Boston homicide department.

Richards displayed an air of complete confidence. He surveyed the trio around him and said, "First time I've been face to face with a homicide man.

Now I get to talk to three at once." He took a seat and asked, "Now, what's this all about?"

Art took the lead in the discussion. "You know all about the robbery and murder last Friday?"

"Yes. First time that's ever happened at a bridge tournament."

"There were about twenty-five thousand dollars stolen at the time."

"So I heard."

"Some of the money was in cash, some in checks, and some in bridge bucks. At the moment, we're trying to trace the bridge bucks."

"That must be a challenge," said Richards, now squinting through his thick glasses.

"It may be. But we have tools like serial numbers and fingerprinting to help us track them. What we'd like from you is information on how you acquired the bridge bucks you're currently using."

"Well, I bought them. Same as anybody else."

"Do you have a receipt?"

"Not on me. But I'm sure it's in my room. I seldom keep the things anyway. I find I can rely pretty much on my credit card company to keep good records. Matter of fact, I think I threw it out."

"Is your room here at the Westin?" asked Julia, participating for the first time.

"Yes, it is," answered Richards. As an afterthought, he blurted, "Why?"

Julia smoothly continued. "I thought, if it was convenient, you could go up and have a quick look for it."

"Well, I can look after the game. I'll let you know."

Art broke in. "Look, Steve. We happen to know that you didn't buy any bridge bucks last Friday. We also know that the serial numbers on the bridge bucks you're using came from the batch sold that Friday and were used to buy entries in the Life Master pairs. So, let's hear again how you acquired your bridge bucks."

"This is a pile of crap. I told you I usually throw out my VISA receipts."

"All we need from you is the information on where you got your bridge bucks," pressed Art.

"You obviously don't understand English."

They concluded with Art telling Richards to go along and enjoy his game. When he had gone, Julia said, "We can get his room number from the front desk. We ought to search his room while he's playing."

Fraser paused for a moment before answering. "I'd really like to go through a few rooms, not just one. Both here and in the Marriott. I know that's a problem, needing warrants with nothing firm to justify them."

Steele asked, "What would you be looking for?"

"Traces of evidence. A ski mask. Dart equipment. Chemicals."

Steele frowned. "Have we got any way to boil down the number of rooms we want to look at? Our D.A. is a huge help. If I don't make brainless requests, he goes along. A warrant for a few rooms I could get, I'm sure. Anything more than that would get in the way of our understanding. Let's lay on something reasonable and avoid provoking a lot of questions."

"How about an open-ended warrant for up to six? Karen and I have a spreadsheet with a list of names that are worth investigating. The list covers people who bought blowguns and supplies over the past year who are also members of the bridge league. We can look at our spreadsheet a little more and come up with something more specific. Not all of the people on our list are in the Westin. Maybe only two or three."

"We just agreed that we have something pretty solid at the Westin. What do we gain by looking in the Marriott?" asked Steele.

Art responded, "There are only a couple more names staying there. If we're going to the trouble of getting a search warrant, let's cover all the bases. We'll spin our wheels if we repeat this several times over. How about a total of five rooms? Three in the Marriott and a couple in the Westin. You said your D.A. is a good guy."

"There are limits. It would help if we knew exactly which rooms you want to break and enter."

"It'll take a little time to fix up a list. The exact rooms can't be that important. You look like a man who can be trusted."

"Okay. So you want it open-ended. Not asking much," said Steele. He took out his cell phone once again, dialed a number, gave his name and asked for Bert to come to the phone right away, if possible.

"I need a special favor, Bert. We want to search a few rooms here but don't know the numbers yet. This has to be a bit open-ended. Maybe five at most. What? I don't like maybes either. Two hotels are involved, the Westin and the Marriott. We're making a spreadsheet now of all the suspects. There aren't that many. We're getting a definite lead on the perp. No, we don't know if he's still in one of the hotels. Okay. Can you fax the warrant over? I'll get you the number in five minutes. Terrific. Yeah, I'll get you a couple of Bruins tickets."

He turned to Art and asked him to get the Westin fax number. "Let's go to the Bulletin office. They have a fax machine in there."

"Bulletin?"

"It's the daily newspaper the bridge league publishes at every national tournament. The office is on this floor. They have all the equipment we need right there."

They found the assistant editor busily working on the next day's edition, along with two of the players who contributed regularly. Art made the necessary arrangements while Steele phoned his contact, and within the hour, they had a copy of a warrant to search five rooms.

"I hope this is good. Bruins tickets are expensive," said Steele.

"How do we work this?" asked Art. "We don't all have to go through all of the rooms. Suppose Julia and I go through the rooms at the Westin and, Bill, you handle the Marriott. Julia's met the housekeeping manager already, so that'll make it easy to get pass keys here. Bill, you'll have to talk to the night manager at the Marriott to get pass keys. I'll have a list of room numbers by the time you're back."

Julia said, "Chris is gonna love us."

"Those are the breaks. If he doesn't like it, maybe he can find a better job. We're not hurting him personally in any way."

"True. Let's go."

"I'll see if he's in." Art called a number and got Chris quickly. "I have a detective from Boston homicide who wants to talk to you."

"Why me? I ain't done nothing. How many detectives you gonna bring around?"

"Ask Julia when she gets there. She'll be right down."

Chris said, "Is she any good with a mop? Why don't you just get her to sign on to my cleaning staff. That'd make it easier for us to talk."

"I'll ask her."

"I don't believe you guys. You gotta give me about half an hour. I got things to do here."

"We're in a hurry. All we want is a master key."

Art hung up and turned back to the group in his room. "Chris says come down in half an hour," Art said. "I told him you'd be right down. I think I've made him nervous by telling him the police are involved. I doubt we'll have any trouble."

"Your call. You know your man best," said Julia.

Fraser told her about the cubby hole on the third floor.

When Julia left, Art went to his room, loaded the spreadsheet on his computer and printed off the names of people staying at the Westin or the Marriott who met the criteria for doing business with Ughdart as well as being ACBL members. He got room numbers through the manager on duty and went back down to the room where Julia and Bill were waiting.

Julia flashed her master keys. "When I showed Chris the warrant, he gave me a set of master keys without any argument at all."

"He's a pussycat, really. He's been helpful all along." He gave Julia a list of the three numbers they were going to enter in the Westin and showed Bill the two numbers he wanted him to search in the Marriott. "We should get this done pretty quickly. Let's meet back here as soon as we're done."

Bill left first and walked through the overpass to the Marriott. He picked up a master key from the night manager and went up to the first room on Fraser's list. He knocked at the door and listened for a response or a sign of activity.

"What can I do for you?" came a female voice.

"Police, ma'am. I need to look over your room," Bill was puzzled by the response. He was sure that Fraser had promised him the rooms would be unoccupied.

"I won't let strangers into my room," said the voice.

"I have a warrant and I'm authorized to enter," he answered.

"Can you come back later?"

"I only need a few minutes of your time."

"I don't know what this is about."

Steele was finished talking. He took out his master key, opened the lock, then took out a second key and opened the security lock. After all this, the door opened six inches and then stopped, held securely by the safety chain. He could hear commotion inside the room. Bill took a tool out of his pocket, smirked, fished around the edge of the door and neatly disconnected the chain on the other side.

He entered the room and found a disheveled woman hurrying to tie the belt on her housecoat. A shirtless, shoeless, pantless man wearing only a black thong sat on the edge of the bed, looking sheepish but satisfied.

"Thank you very much," said the woman. "What happened to privacy? I'm going to call the police."

Bill remained perfectly composed. "I am the police. Detective Bill Steele, Boston homicide. I need a quick look around. Here's my warrant," he said, waving a copy of the faxed paper. The document could have been a replica of the Magna Carta as far as the couple were concerned, since neither the man nor the woman had ever seen a warrant. Still, they were sufficiently impressed to stand aside as Bill took a look through the room. When he was satisfied that one small handbag, the closet, drawers and cupboards, bathroom and bed contained nothing of interest, he bade farewell to the occupants.

"You must be investigating the murder and robbery."

"I am. We thought everyone would have been playing."

"We're sitting out this round. We have six on our team."

"I'm not sure what you mean," said Bill. "Sorry to trouble you, but we need to cover all the ground we can."

"I don't know what in hell you expected to find in here."

They left it at that and Bill moved on.

Meanwhile, Julia and Art went through two unoccupied rooms in the Westin and found nothing. The remaining room was the one belonging to Richards. Thankfully, the room was unoccupied. They surveyed the room quickly and, seeing nothing obvious, opened all of the drawers in the various cabinets in the room. They carefully inspected the luggage, took the blankets and sheets off the bed, inspected the pillows, and found nothing. "Any good at making beds?" asked Julia.

Art smirked and replied, "I've had lessons but I'm out of practice. Let's go."

They quickly restored the bed to its professionally made appearance. The pair once again went through the room, more thoroughly this time than the first and again came up empty. The room had been cleaned and tidied and only the luggage plus a few items in the closet marked the sign of a lodger. They were on the verge of abandoning the room when Julia said, "Maybe he's a cook."

"What do you mean by that?" asked Art.

Julia, without answering, opened the door of the microwave and then closed it, muttering, "Nope." When she opened the door of the small refrigerator, she called out, "Well, well." Art came over to inspect what Julia had found. Lying on a shelf was a neatly packed white plastic laundry bag with Westin prominently printed on it.

"Find something interesting?" asked Art.

"A neat little bag of something," said Julia. "Too neat."

Art bent down and caught a glimpse of yellow paper inside the bag. "Bridge bucks," said Art. "And some checks. Bingo."

Art retrieved the bag with a gloved hand. They laid it carefully on the bed. Julia took out her digital camera and began snapping pictures. Art was silent for a few moments, absorbed in looking through the bag to estimate the size of the cache. He flipped open his notebook to check the serial numbers of currency sold on the first day of the tournament. The bills he was looking at fell within the range Alan had provided. "This has to be part of the haul the perp made off with. There are several thousand bridge bucks here. At least three or four thousand. And a lot of checks as well. No cash, but this wad probably accounts for the balance of five thousand that was stolen."

"Beats me how you find a pile of five thousand bucks," said Julia. "Even if it's all checks and funny money, that's a big sum to leave behind."

"The robber has twenty thousand real bucks to spend—plenty of cash to pay for a room for several nights. It was probably necessary to leave the bridge bucks behind. To anyone except a regular player, the paper would be more of a burden than an asset. These bridge bucks are only useful in small quantities. An entry costs seventy-two dollars if you play in a pairs game or a hundred-and-forty-four for a team game. The bridge bucks don't come in smaller denominations. Twenty bucks is the smallest unit. People have to use a multiple of twenty that's close to the entry fee and either take change or make up the balance. Any player trying to dispose of a larger wad, like a thousand dollars' worth or more, would arouse immediate suspicion. Now that we've got serial numbers for the bills, it'd be especially dangerous. Same thing with the checks. If he tried to use them, it would be like calling the cops on himself. Maybe he was hoping they'd remain in this room unnoticed for a few days."

"Or he may have left in a big hurry. By the way, we can get prints from that stuff," said Julia. "Be careful handling it."

"In case you didn't notice, I'm wearing gloves," said Art. "We'd better have another talk with our friend Richards. His match finishes shortly after ten. We can get him then and grill him."

"Hey, why should we wait? This is urgent." Julia was excited now.

Art responded, "Look. If we pull him out of the game, we ruin it for everybody in the event. He's not going anywhere. We'll go down and keep an eye on him and get him as soon as he finishes the round."

"I hope you know what you're doing."

"If he was going to split, he'd be long gone by now. We'll go down to the ballroom shortly after ten and wait for him. We'll bring him up to a conference room for questioning."

"My, how I trust you. Should I?"

"Let me know if you can find a better way," Art laughed. "Ten-fifteen will come pretty soon. How about letting Bill know what we're up to."

"I wonder what happened to the immobilization junk. You know, the darts and chemicals that he used? Where would he have left them?" wondered Julia.

"He probably flushed the chemicals down the sink and broke up the blow tubes and threw them in the garbage."

They left the room as neat as they had found it, took the refrigerated bag full of checks and ACBL currency, and went to meet Bill. Art told him about the plan to meet Richards in the playing room just after ten o'clock.

Dot Jefe called just before ten that night. "I had a visit with an old school friend," she said. "Haven't seen her for years. We went out to dinner and yakked for hours. How's your investigation coming?"

"Terrible," said Art. "But that's normal for this stage of a case. Tell me, we want to get in touch with a caddy named Bobby Rideau. How do we do that?"

"That's going to be a challenge," said Dot. "Bobby's not around anymore."

"What do you mean, not around?"

"He was here for a day. He worked the North American pairs game on Thursday. Afternoon and night. Then he just didn't show up. We always have a number of standbys available, and we called in a replacement."

"Didn't Bobby wait to get paid?"

"Oh yes. Our policy is to pay cash every day. These caddies live hand to mouth, and they wouldn't survive if they didn't have cash."

"So Bobby worked just one day and then disappeared?"

"That's right."

"Is there a way of contacting him?"

"He left a Boston address and phone number. Come by my desk tomorrow and I'll give you what I've got. This was our first time hiring Bobby, and I can't guarantee the accuracy of our records. When I think about it, I could probably guarantee that it's useless. The guy's obviously not reliable. Some of our caddies have been with us for several tournaments, a year or two. Others are known to the locals. But not Bobby. He was a stranger. I interviewed him myself. He impressed me to start with—well-mannered, well-spoken, neat. Nothing he did raised any alarm bells. Just the opposite, in fact. But we knew nothing about his background.”

“Thanks, Dot. Can I come by at eight-thirty tomorrow?”

“That’s early.”

“I’ll have at least one Boston homicide detective with me.”

“Well, okay. Come on down. Room eight-seven-five.”

“See you then. And thanks.”

Art went directly to the ballroom after talking to Dot. He spotted Julia and Bill talking quietly just outside the ballroom. He couldn’t work out whether they were nervous, impatient, or both. “Ready to talk to Mr. Richards?” he asked.

“I hope he’s still in town.”

Art surveyed the playing area and couldn’t spot him. He walked over to the directors table and asked for help finding Steve Richards. “Section BB, table twelve,” was the answer. Art gazed in that direction and spotted their man.

“He’s right over there,” he said to Julia, pointing over the heads of a mass of people.

“This reminds me of golf,” said Julia. “One person in the foursome knows where everybody’s balls go and nobody else can see them.”

“They’ll be finished shortly,” said Art. “While we’re waiting, I have a lead on a name, Bobby Rideau, that’s beginning to look promising. Evidently he’s a dead match for the face in Karsh’s composite. It may well be an alias, but that’s what we have to go on at the moment. This person applied for a job here at the tournament. They hired him, but he only stuck around for one day. He’s been a no show since. He left a Boston address and phone number. I think it would be worth our while to take a trip to that address and look around for signs of activity. It may be a complete fake, but it could be a true lead. For all we know, he may still be staying there. If we can track him down, we may have something.”

Julia thought it a good idea to visit the address immediately. *I wonder what immediately means in Boston*, thought Art.

“I don’t have an address yet,” he said. “First thing I want to do tomorrow is meet with the person in charge of caddies. That’s set for eight-thirty tomorrow morning. Care to join me?” He was pleased when Julia agreed to the meeting, and downright ecstatic when she also agreed to drive him out to the suburbs once he had an address.

Art pointed to the table where Richards was sitting. "They're finished playing now," said Art. "Let's go."

Richards wore a white turtleneck under his blue suit, and his partner had on a grey suit, white shirt and a reddish-striped silk tie. They stood out in a crowd where the players were casually or in many cases sloppily dressed. Art moved to intercept Steve Richards as he got up from his table. "Could you join us, Steve?" asked Art. "We want to run over a couple of things with you."

"We haven't compared scores yet. I'd like to see how we finished," responded Richards. "I think we beat them. They're supposed to be a good team, too. What's this anyway?"

"We need to talk about bridge bucks."

"We already did that. I don't have time for more of that crap."

Julia spoke up. "I think you'll make time. We can talk down at headquarters if you prefer."

Richards snapped his chin up. "Just let us compare scores and then we'll see."

Art nodded to Julia and Bill that this was okay. "They just finished a match. It'll only take a couple of minutes to get their scores. I'd feel the same way in his boots."

After a few moments, Richards came over to where they were standing, his face looking grim. He had his partner in tow. "Ed is coming along."

"We only need you," said Art.

"Ed's my lawyer. You guys are getting serious and I need support."

Art looked at Julia and Bill, who shrugged as though there was nothing to prevent Richard's move. He introduced everyone. The attorney identified himself as Ed Muster from Chicago. Art said, "We're going down to the third floor. We have a private meeting room there." He led the way, with Julia and Bill trailing behind the group. Once inside the conference room, Art motioned them all to take chairs.

Art reviewed the role he and Julia were playing in the investigation of the robbery and murder that had taken place on the previous Friday. He noted that there had been approximately four thousand dollars in bridge bucks involved in the robbery. "Steve was using bucks with serial numbers corresponding to those sold on Friday, before the Life Masters pairs game. They were part of the loot taken during the robbery."

Muster gave Richards a sharp look, then addressed Art and Julia. "So what? I don't see where that takes us."

"That takes us nowhere," agreed Art. "We had a warrant to search Steve's room tonight and guess what? We found the whole stash of stolen ACBL currency. That's what we want to talk about. I suppose that's why he brought you along."

Muster again turned a steady gaze on Richards. "Steve, you don't have to answer a damned thing here if you don't want to. I have no idea what this is all about, but I do know your rights. You can exercise them if you choose."

Art interrupted. "You certainly can keep mum. But consider the whole scene we have here. We don't know how you came across this stash of money. It was in the refrigerator in your room. You obviously knew all about it. You used some. One-hundred-and-forty bucks yesterday, and two bunches of eighty bucks today. You came across stolen goods. You didn't report them. You made use of them. If we hadn't caught up with you, you probably would have used all of them. Now what we've got here is a minor crime. Use of stolen goods. If you insist on clamming up and refuse to cooperate, Julia may want to take you over to police headquarters and book you as an accessory. A couple of days in the slammer may change your mind."

"Hang on," said Muster. "We're going too fast. This is the first I've heard about it. Steve and I haven't talked about this at all. Can you give us ten minutes alone?"

"Make it five," said Art. "We'll be out in the hall."

Julia and Bill seemed happy to follow Art's lead. When they were alone, Art asked, "How do you feel about offering some sort of immunity if he cooperates? I suspect he found the money, but didn't steal it. I'm pretty sure he had nothing to do with the actual robbery and killing."

Bill responded, "That makes sense to me. I should run it by the D.A.'s office."

"At this time of night?"

"You're right. I'll have to use some weasel words and waffle a bit. I want to make sure the offer of immunity extends only to possession and use of stolen goods. If we come across other misdemeanors, we'll have to hold him responsible."

"Good points, all of them. Muster must understand our problem about granting immunity without touching base with the D.A. Let's play it out this way."

Bill said, "Let me handle the discussion when they come back. I think I know what to say when the issue of immunity comes up."

Julia and Art nodded agreement. Muster came to the door and announced they were ready to continue. He said, "You were eloquent on the subject of making threats about accessories. Let's hear other options."

Bill took the lead at this point. "Mr. Richards here knows how he came by the stolen property. We'd like him to share that knowledge with us."

"Supposing he does?"

"We might consider dropping any charges related to possession and use of stolen goods, which Mr. Richards is obviously guilty of."

"Might consider? That's not much of a promise. Can you do better?"

"Depends on what the benefits are."

"Alright. If you agree to drop charges completely, we'll agree to provide you with information on how this unfortunate set of affairs transpired."

"We might drop charges related to possession and use. If we find Mr. Richards has committed some other felony, we'd have to hold him responsible for that. We don't know yet how he came across the notes."

"That's not much of a concession. You don't even know if your D.A. will back you up."

"He'll have no choice."

"Alright. We have a deal. Steve, go ahead and tell these people what happened."

"You sure you know what we're doing?" asked Richards.

"If you have a better idea, go ahead and try it," said an exasperated Muster.

"Okay. I checked into this room on Saturday. I played bridge all day, and next morning, I go to check for an empty laundry bag. I look up on the shelf and pull this bag down. Only, it's not empty. It's lying flat, not bulging at all, like you might expect. I pull the thing down and I see a bunch of yellow paper sticking out. I find it's full of neatly packed bridge bucks. Like a fool, I decide to keep it and use it. That's all there is to it."

Art asked, "What about all of the checks made out to the ACBL? Would you be happy to see the league lose over a thousand bucks for nothing?"

Richards made a few spluttering noises and Muster added, "There's no point in adding schoolboy lectures to all of this. We're now all aware of exactly what happened. I suggest we adjourn. You have your money and your checks."

Art nodded. "Julia will need sample fingerprints. We may have some follow-up questions later."

Richards complained, "I don't see why you need lousy fingerprints and I don't see why any further questions will help anything. You've got what you wanted."

Muster broke in. "Steve, let's go along with these people. They've got a major crime to solve and we should be helping them as much as we can. You're clear. Let's give them your prints. Then we'll shut up and get out."

"One more item," said Art. "You owe the ACBL three hundred bucks to make up for the stolen goods."

Richards reddened and started to protest. Muster gave him a solemn look. "You mean you bought our entry with this currency and then collected from your teammates?"

Richards spluttered some more and eventually nodded. Muster took his wallet out and, without a word, laid bills on the table in front of him. He led the way out.

When they were alone again, Art said, "Let's go down to the front desk and find out who was using that room Friday."

The trio marched off to the Westin lobby and contacted the night manager. Art said, "We need to know who was renting room five-fifty-five last Friday night. Maybe nights before that as well, but definitely Friday."

The manager led them into his office, woke up his computer, and began scrolling for the information. "Here we go. The room was rented to a Bobby Rainbow, Portland, Oregon. I'll print you off all of the information."

"We need credit card information as well," said Julia.

"Sorry. No credit card. The room was prepaid in cash." He handed Julia a sheet of paper. "One copy enough?"

Art said, "That's plenty. Thanks."

Bill said, "While we're here, how about walking through the scene of the crime. I'd like to get a first-hand feel for exactly what took place. It won't take long."

"Good idea," said Art. "I've been over the territory a dozen times, but once more won't hurt. How about you Julia?"

"It's past my bedtime anyway," she answered. "Another couple of hours won't make a difference."

Art contacted the night manager once again and alerted him to their plan. They took the elevator to the ballroom floor and found that while there were a few tables engaged in a midnight Swiss game, otherwise everything was quiet.

Art had an eerie feeling as they entered the ballroom where the Life Masters Pairs game had been held. He ran the detectives over the route that the killer had taken—the place where entries had been sold, the exact spot where the immobilization darts had been launched and the route the killer would have taken on his way out.

"This had to be a one-man show," said Art. "I can't see more than one person handling this without being spotted. It's a miracle that no one can tell us about our suspect anyway."

They paced off the distances involved. The men's and ladies' washrooms were adjacent, about a hundred steps to the area where the entries were sold.

Art continued, "A gap this short could be covered in less than a minute. He'd only need a few minutes in each washroom to place and light the fireworks devices that caused all the racket and started the small fires. That had to happen about half an hour to an hour before game time, according to what Papan and Jose told us. He must have had an idea of the cleaning schedule. Maybe he observed the pair for a few days, or maybe he stopped by Chris' office and looked at his clipboard. Once he knew the time when there'd be no traffic in the washrooms, he'd know when it was safe to step in and install his little surprises. So, he waited until the cleaning routine started, made sure traffic to the washroom stopped completely, and then placed his devices at the bottom of each paper basket, where it would ignite whatever paper happened to be in there. In fact, he probably included some paper along with his fireworks charges to make sure he would have a fire. Maybe some smoke generators as well."

Julia spoke up. "The fireworks store that I visited reported that somebody bought a couple of smoke generators along with a bunch of noisy firecrackers. That was probably our man."

"They'd be more effective in creating smoke than a small bit of paper and they're readily available," agreed Art. "Of course, the estimate of a minute or so from the washroom to the ballroom floor is meaningless. The killer must have been keeping an eye on things for at least an hour before pandemonium exploded. How could he get close to the tables where entries were being sold without being noticed? His face would likely be familiar to the directors. He would have planned his activities so no attention would be drawn to him and no suspicions aroused. He couldn't have been standing around or interfering with the work the bridge staff were doing. He must have timed his approach to coincide with the exact few seconds when chaos erupted."

"A pretty cool customer," said Bill. "His first step was to get everyone in a frenzy with fireworks explosions and a couple of small fires. Then he had to have mass commotion as the hotel evacuation system got set off. Then what?"

Art said, "While everyone was panicking and focusing on obeying evacuation instructions, he slipped on a ski mask and stunned two directors. Then he walked off with the money. All that must have been worked out in detail and executed without a hitch."

Bill said, "There was a hitch alright. He killed someone. He certainly didn't plan that."

"For sure. That's a case of manslaughter," agreed Art. "Both Papan and Jose say they saw him just a few minutes before the game, wearing a hotel outfit. What did he do with the clothes he got rid of?"

"You're sure he didn't have a job on the cleaning staff?" asked Bill.

"That would have been a logical move, come to think of it," said Art. "We showed Chris the composite drawing and discussed the whole matter with him at length."

"Maybe you should have offered him some money," smiled Julia.

"Don't make me nervous," said Art. "I hope Chris isn't holding anything back. We'll have to recycle that one. Anyway, there's no doubt the perp had to get his hands on a decent-fitting hotel uniform. Bridge players are so focused on their game and their partners that they often don't notice what's happening around them. And the directors wouldn't have paid any attention to a hotel employee casually doing odd jobs in the ballroom, even if the person was a stranger."

"It sounds like Papan and Jose didn't pay much attention to him either," said Steele. "He must have had a couple of outfits—a hotel uniform and regular clothes. And he needed a place to change."

Bill nodded and said, "He would've had to get from the ballroom to his room without raising suspicion. It wouldn't be that hard to do."

Art said, "And the only change of clothing needed would have been a shirt because in reality uniform means shirt. Caddies and directing staff sometimes wear uniforms, but they're really just shirts. Trousers, slacks, don't matter. People wear trousers of any description, but the shirts they wear are neat and at least have a rough resemblance to a uniform."

"That probably applies to hotel cleaning staff as well," said Bill.

"That's true," said Art. "He did his work in the ladies' washroom first, then set up the fireworks in the men's washroom, and went on to his crime."

Julia said, "He would've needed a good big bag to carry all of his tools—fireworks and blowguns—and the money afterwards. The killer had to get out of the room with the money. How could he do that? One of the hotel employees would likely have noticed a laggard hanging back once the signal to evacuate sounded."

Art said, "There's a coat rack just outside the door to the ballroom. He could easily have left a coat there for the purpose of grabbing it on the way out and totally covering the clothing he was wearing. He wouldn't have had to change at all."

"Would the whole hotel have been ordered to evacuate?" wondered Julia.

"Definitely not," replied Bill. "They'd never get all of the guests out of their rooms. There must be over eight hundred rooms here—a thousand people at least, not all bridge players. The hotel staff would just concern themselves with the floor where the problem was identified. So all the killer had to do was get to another floor, quickly. Then he'd be safe, for the moment, and able to pursue the next step, which would be to disappear with a bag of money."

The trio walked over to the bank of six elevators on the ballroom floor. Right in behind the elevators, there was a door marked **EMPLOYEES ONLY**. They looked in and saw a group of service elevators, normally used only by hotel staff.

Julia said, "Here's what our friend used, I'll bet. The whole place was chaos and I'll bet he just walked over here, unnoticed, through these doors, into a service elevator, and disappeared quickly to the fifth floor and his room."

Bill observed, "He had all of these details worked out, it seems."

"Where does this leave us?" Art asked. "We knew we were chasing a smart criminal. He must have been totally familiar with the hotel layout. Everyone who was buying or had just bought an entry could have seen him. We pasted the police artist's drawing onto the front page of the Bulletin. Why wasn't there more reaction to it? He must have dressed in such a way so as not to draw attention. There must be something, some feature that's vastly different between the actual face and what Papan and Jose think they saw in the washrooms."

"Disguises can be bought," offered Julia. "A little skill goes a long way."

"I notice you have video cameras set up in the ballroom? Are they used a lot?" asked Bill.

Art answered, "The league's been using video cameras for a couple of years now. Generally, they're in use when the game is on in some of the sessions. It's possible there were some running here at the time of the robbery. If they captured any action just at game time, it could be very useful indeed. We'd better look into that. I'll get that going first thing tomorrow."

Julia smiled, "Did we say something about not taking two hours? Our time will be up in five minutes."

Bill said, "We'd better catch an hour of sleep before it's too late."

"About tomorrow morning. I still have that date with Dot Jefe. She the one who looks after the caddies—hires them, fires them, pays them and generally looks after them. Julia, remember you said you wanted to come along? Eight-thirty."

"I'll be there."

It was after two a.m. when Art finished and went to the bedroom in their suite. As he entered, Clive tested his lungs, signaling that he was hungry and wet.

Karen turned over sleepily. "Did you win the midnight game?" she muttered.

Art laughed. "I've been tracing bridge bucks. We found them. Positively." He related the story of the meeting with Richards and Muster. He changed Clive and brought him to Karen so that she could deal with the remaining necessities.

CHAPTER 8

BRUCE LENTE ROSE THURSDAY MORNING, overcame momentary disorientation, and realized he was in the Omaha Airport Marriott. As a result of his snap decision to travel to Omaha from Boston, he had not gone home after work the previous day. Instead, he'd had his secretary make travel arrangements while he phoned his wife, and then left his downtown office for Logan airport. The briefcase he carried had little in it except for a couple of interesting magazines and his file on the *BOSTON BRIDGE MURDER* case. When he checked in, he realized that he needed certain necessities for a clean start the next day. Luckily, the front desk obliged him with shaving utensils and tooth-cleaning supplies. He made use of them. He didn't mind wearing the same clothes two days in a row. He had done worse, many times, in the marines. John Marshall was waiting for him when he arrived at the Omaha police station and offered coffee and donuts.

"Hold the donuts, John. The Marriott provides a pretty good breakfast. I'll take the coffee though."

"Probably a good idea. I made reservations for lunch at Sebastian's steak house. I'll bet you never get decent beef in Boston."

"Do they have beer on tap?"

"Only thirty or forty brands. Don't forget, the man on expense account pays the bill.

"I knew you'd say that."

"Tell me about your man, Ruhe."

"We had a man killed at a hotel downtown. There was a big bridge tournament on and the victim was a guy handling the money. The murder weapon was a blowgun firing the kind of immobilization dart that veterinarians use to handle animals. Ever come across them?"

"Not exactly. I've seen the rifles that zoo keepers use. And the darts. Are they the same?"

"The dart is similar, but a blowgun's a small unit. It's compact, easy to hide, and quiet. It doesn't have a big range, but if you're two feet away from your target, you don't need range. It can be deadly. Getting back to Ruhe, he's a veterinarian and a bridge player. He was in Boston for a the tournament over the weekend. Take a look at this." He showed Marshall the drawing that Karsh had created. "I had a police artist in Boston make this up. You know the drill—get witnesses to tell you about his features, try a few times and get something they think looks like the perp. This is what he came up with. Danged if somebody that knows this guy Ruhe doesn't show up and claim that he's an exact match for the person in the picture. Before we get to talk to him, Ruhe disappears from Boston, leaving no trail and no explanation. The interesting thing here is that Ruhe was a customer of Ughdart—the outfit that sells the animal immobilizers. He bought several blowguns and plenty of darts over the past few years."

"So Mr. Ruhe is your number one suspect right now. Sounds like a good candidate. Let's go find out about him."

Lente and Marshall sipped their coffee while discussing plans. Marshall said, "We must have a hundred veterinarians in Omaha. Probably a dozen Ruhes. We ought to be able to pin this down quickly." He rose to pick up two phone books from a table. "I'll give you the easy one," he said as he gave the yellow pages to Lente.

"You're slick," said Lente, burying himself in the tome. Minutes later, he reported, "Here it is. I'm sure this must be the one. Pet Clinic, T. Ruhe, DVM." Lente read out the address.

"I've got a residence for a T. Ruhe here as well. That's gotta be the guy," said Marshall. "Make a note of these addresses. Let's go over to yours first. We can try the one I got if we strike out at the vet's place."

"Maybe we'll have to do both anyway," said Lente. "Think the vet will be open already?"

"It'll be after nine by the time we get there. He'll be open," responded Marshall.

The two officers finished their coffee, hopped into Marshall's police sedan and headed for the address that Lente had recorded.

~  ~

Art awoke at eight, groggy from his lack of sleep but energized with adrenaline. He remembered his meetings and pushed himself to get moving. Julia called at eight-fifteen a.m. and Art went down to the lobby after checking with Dot. He took Julia up to Dot's room. "I checked with Dot Jefe—that's the person you're going to meet in a minute. She says she's ready for us. She hires and fires the caddies."

"I didn't know you needed people to carry golf clubs around at a bridge tournament," said Julia.

Art smiled. "Sorry. At a bridge tournament, there are simple jobs that need doing, like carrying score slips from the tables up to the chief director's desk. They also run errands for the directors and players, move furniture around, and generally do any odd jobs that come along. Dot gets to know the regulars quite well."

When they arrived at Dot's room, she had her computer running and she looked up Bobby Rideau, then printed off the data she had. "It's not much," she said. "Just a local address and a phone number. I haven't even checked either out. I tried the phone number he gave us, but got no answer. I hired a replacement for him right away from our waiting group."

"He never did show up again?"

"No," said Dot. "If he had, I wouldn't have used him again. If someone is reliable, I work with him. When someone stands me up, unless they apologize and have a good story, they're done with me."

Art entered the phone number and address into his notebook.

Julia asked, "How do you recruit these people?"

Dot replied, "Mostly caddies are hired by referrals. Either they're teenage relatives of players picking up allowance supplements, or older folks who need a little cash and are happy to do the job. They're always known to some player who gives them a reference. Sometimes the tournament organizers know a few locals who need money badly and are willing to do caddy work. The pay is strictly minimum wage, and they're paid at the end of every day. When a person like Rideau walks in, applies for a job, charms everyone for a few minutes, shows some energy, he lands the job. He did a good job the first day, but didn't return the second or third day. He just didn't show up. We can't even be sure of his name. It's the one he gave when he applied for a job."

Julia said, "Beats me how you bridge folks are so casual about your relationships. You really do a thorough job vetting your prospective employees."

Dot replied, "Don't we, though. There's certainly no big interview program. Try working with the minimum wage group sometime. The reason why folks are in that group is that that's all they're worth. They're either kids just starting in the work force, with no experience, or older people who have a bad work history. They might even have some problem like no experience, unreliability, alcohol, you name it. They can be elderly, unemployed, sometimes otherwise unemployable. That's all fine with us. As long as they're honest and reliable for the few days they're with us.

"There's no long term commitment by either side. If a caddy doesn't work out for any reason—behavior, manners, dress habits, anything at all—we just tell them not to bother coming back the next day."

Julia nodded. "It's a different world," she said. "Mind you, every case I work comes with its own world."

The detectives thanked Dot and left for their meeting room. Art got no answer when he tried the phone number Dot had given him. Julia set up her laptop and traced the name of the couple at the address. "The home is evidently owned by a retired couple," she said. "John and Ann Graham. They're in their seventies, both of them. No doubt retired."

"They're likely not in Boston right now. Presumably traveling. They may be in Florida," said Art.

"Does their name ring a bell? Is there a possible relationship with Rideau?"

"Don't know," responded Art. "The Graham name doesn't click with me, but then neither does Rideau."

"Do you get the feeling we're on swampy ground here? The name Bobby Rideau may or may not be fictitious. Ditto for the address. Our man might have pulled the name, address and phone number out of a hat and never really knew the folks at that address. Or he could have been using the place as his own headquarters with or without the knowledge of the owners."

"We have to check all those things out. We'd better pay a visit to Thorncrest Avenue," said Art.

"I'm all for that. Do you have a copy of Karsh's picture? We could show it to the neighbors."

"I wouldn't be without it. Come to think of it, we ought to be plugging the picture into your police computer and testing for a match. And maybe get it to the FBI and into their computer to do a national search. It's possible this isn't Mr. Rideau's first experiment with unlawful activity."

Julia said, "We've already run it through our Boston database. Nothing showed up there. I'll set up a contact with the FBI."

Art went back to his suite to touch base with Karen and pick up the thin cotton jacket he had brought as his only defense against Boston weather. "Julia and I are off to the suburbs to check out an address that the caddy gave to Dot. We'll talk to some of the neighbors as well."

"That sounds like fun. Want to borrow my coat?"

"I'd never get the buttons done up. Listen, I had another thought today."

"Keep doing that. It'll help your reputation."

"You know the security cameras the ACBL has installed?"

"All I know is the information they've circulated. They're saying that video recording is going to start at some point."

"Well, they're recording on a regular basis now. Maybe you could talk to Fred Jardeen about it. I'm not sure if it's done on a professional basis or if it's still experimental, but cameras are out there. Records are being made, and they're stored for a time. If there's a suspicious incident, the records are looked at. In some cases, they'll focus the cameras on a specific player, or his table."

"I see," said Karen. "And you're hoping they may have picked up something the day of the robbery."

"Exactly. There may have been coverage of the area where money was taken in. It'll be a fluke if there was. They normally start rolling only after the game is underway. And then they focus on the playing area, not the directors' desks. But it's a lead we can't overlook. We're going to get lucky one of these times," said Art. "So far, the people we are most interested in are leaving town."

"I can get hold of Fred while you're out on your date."

"Don't talk about dates with Julia to me. She's the last person I'd ask for a date."

"You mean there are others besides me?" pouted Karen.

"Oh yes. Many, many. It just that Julia isn't one of them.

Art went down to the vehicle loading area just outside the lobby and found that Julia had retrieved her car and was waiting. They headed for the address on Thorncrest Avenue. Traffic reduced to a trickle as they got further into the suburbs of Boston. Thorncrest was a short street of small, neat brick bungalows. No doubt it was beautiful in spring and summer, but in late November, under grey skies, it was lined with leafless maple trees that looked vaguely like a group of headless skeletons. The odd numbers were on the left.

When they reached number 59, Julia pulled her Dodge Charger into the laneway and they got out. The bungalow looked deserted, but the grounds were tidy. A quick look around the exterior of the house revealed there was no sign of forced entry or damage anywhere. All of the doors and windows were secure. Anyone using the home had to have used a key for entry.

"Let's ask a few neighbors if they've seen anything," said Julia.

"Your badge will come in handy. Not many people want to talk to a private eye."

"Nice to be appreciated," smiled Julia. "Even if it is for the wrong thing."

Art noted the smile, the first that she had flashed in his company. *Keep it going,* he thought. Art was pleased to find that their rapport had taken a giant step forward. He needed that, and he needed it to continue.

He and Julia called on the nearest neighbors. They discovered life in the second house. A white-haired lady opened the door a crack, saw Julia, and said, "No thanks. I don't need any today." She started to close the door.

Julia was wearing a stout pair of walking shoes and had developed a pretty good maneuver with her foot to take care of such situations. She managed to stop the closure, but had not counted on the force of the elderly owner's effort. She winced, flashed her badge, and, for the second time in a half hour, a smile. "We're inquiring about the property at fifteen-nineteen," she said. "Do you know the Grahams?"

The lady squinted at the badge, caught a glimpse of Art, and brightened. "I didn't see you there. Come in. I'm Grace Mayores." She shook hands with her two visitors, and began to open up. "Oh yes," she said. "The Grahams. They're my neighbors. John and Ann Graham. They're in Florida just now. They won't be back until Christmas."

"Do they ever give the key to anyone?"

"Yes, I have a key."

"Is anyone allowed to enter the property? To stay, or to do repair work?"

"Not that I know of. They don't have children. Oh, unless you count their niece. They took her in when she was a teenager. She's a wild one. She hardly ever comes here now. I think they get together in Florida."

"You haven't seen anyone within the last two or three days?"

"No, I'm sorry. I go over every morning. Usually about ten."

"Do you go in and look around?"

"Oh my, no. I just walk around the house, check the mail and make sure there's no papers or flyers lying around. I check for break-ins as well. This is a pretty peaceful neighborhood."

"You said you have a key. Could we use it?"

"Yes, I do. I suppose I could let you have it." She turned to address Art. "You are from the police? Do you mind telling me what the trouble is?"

Art took his cue. "There's no trouble that we know of. Not yet, anyway. A person we're investigating gave this address. We have a drawing of the person we're looking for."

"I'll bet that's the niece," said Grace. Art unfolded his copy of the picture from the front page of a Bulletin.

"Here."

"Oh my. That does look like the niece. Except that's a boy, er, a man. Anyway it's not her, but there is a resemblance. I think you're looking for the wrong person. I haven't seen the niece recently."

"We have to be thorough," said Art. "Does the name Bobby Rideau mean anything to you?"

"Oh no. I told you they have a niece. Her name is Barbara. I forget her last name, but I know it wasn't Rideau."

"Well, we'd better have a look around anyway."

Grace seemed satisfied and produced a key. "That's for the front door. The storm door isn't locked. You only need the one key. Let me know if there's anything I can do to help. And don't forget to return the key when you're done."

Art and Julia thanked her and left to inspect the Graham home. They entered, looked around, and saw a tidy house with warm, sparkling clean, old-fashioned furnishings in every room. The spotless kitchen showed no sign of recent use. A search of the two bedrooms revealed nothing. The basement shelves were piled high with memorabilia.

"We won't go through this," said Art.

"I guess not. That's about it," said Julia. "Blind trail."

"Looks that way," responded Art. "I'd like one last look in the bedrooms. If our man used any part of the property, one of those would be his first choice."

"Lead on," sighed Julia.

This time, Art looked under beds, in chests of drawers, and in closets. Finally, in one of the closets, at the end of a row of ladies' clothing, a yellow shirt caught his eye. "What's this?" he muttered.

He carefully removed a hanger containing a shirt that was identical to those worn by employees of the Westin. The material and the dull yellow color were similar, and the name WESTIN embroidered on the front confirmed what they had found. "Here we go. Bobby was here," he said to Julia. "The cleaning staff at the Westin wear these shirts. Our friend was definitely here."

"Good," said Julia. "I think it's good. Now what?"

"Obviously Bobby spent a couple of days here, at least. Then he cleared out. That suggests he's not from Boston. What we might do, if you're willing, is go over this garment in detail for prints and DNA. Then we'd have a positive characterization of our suspect when we do come across him."

"I'm willing," said Julia. "That won't be a problem. By the way, you heard the Mayores lady talk about a niece."

"I did," admitted Art.

"That confirms what we've found through your bridge money. The person who rented the room with the bag of money and checks registered as Bobby Rainbow. Bobby Rainbow. Bobby Rideau. Could be the same person. Or it could be the niece. She said Barbara was the niece's name. Let's remember that."

"What's in a name?" asked Art. "Our suspect could have used any number of names."

On the way back to the hotel, Art tried to make sure that Julia was aware of all of the details of the case that he and Karen had dug up, and what the status was of their work. He hoped that Julia would do the same for him. He explained that they were looking into a dozen or so names of people who had purchased blowguns during the past six months.

"Let's talk to Karen back at the hotel. We'll see what progress she's made, and then work out where we're going."

~  ~

Meanwhile, Karen had arranged a meeting with Fred Jardeen to review the subject of security cameras. She needed to deal with Clive for the next hour. Finally, she decided to take him with her. *Fred and the others may not like it, but I have no choice. I'm not hiring a baby sitter I don't know—I don't care if the hotel recommends her.* She bathed Clive, put on fresh clothes, put her sling over her neck and Clive in the sling. He was grinning. *You're beautiful*, she thought. *Just beautiful.*

Fred raised his eyebrows when she showed up with Clive, but he carried on as though it were nothing out of the ordinary.

"What system does he play?" smiled Fred.

"Everything is natural," answered Karen. "He hasn't learned any conventions yet."

Fred explained the camera setup. "The cameras are fairly new. This all started out as a hobby thing, not handled on a professional basis. A couple of enthusiastic directors had good equipment suitable for tests. They also had real know-how and they offered to run some experiments. Their trials were quite successful and, in fact, uncovered a couple of marginal situations that we were able to follow up on. The board has been so concerned about the impact of cheating on the game, especially in important national championships, that they authorized us to allocate professional staff to record and review on a regular basis. That's costing plenty.

"Actually, recording doesn't eat up the man hours; it's the monitoring that does. We can automate the recording part. But if you record a four-hour session, and you want to review it all, someone has to have three to four hours to go through it. We typically have four cameras going through one of these sessions, one on every side of the room. The operators can use software to focus them anywhere in the room. We have two operators working the equipment every session. They've been trained in what to look for, and they focus the cameras at random throughout the session, move them around to different tables, and see what's happening. If they notice anything suspicious, they focus on the same table for a while until they're sure there's a problem, or that everything's clear. If they think they see a problem, they let the head director know. If we have a report of some funny goings-on, we zero in and record maybe a whole session at one table. We've had some remarkable success with the cameras."

"What are our chances that we could find something about last Friday afternoon?"

"Slim. Very slim in fact. But not impossible. The cameras are turned on just before the game and they focus on the playing area. We don't usually bother with the zone where entries are sold. It may be too much to hope that we had a machine pointed at the table where entry fees were being collected. It'd be a real fluke. But I'll talk to our guys and find out. I'll call them right now. Hang on."

"That's impressive," said Karen. "I like that. Thanks."

"My pleasure," said Fred. He dialed the number of Eric Bolls, a director who lived near Rochester, New York. Eric was an amateur photographer of great skill, and had lately taken up a love affair with digital video cameras. He connected on the first ring and Eric was agreeable to coming right up to the office Fred was using. Fred asked him if he could bring along the memory chip used on Friday afternoon, as well as some means to view the videos.

"We'll need a computer that can take a flash drive. Any old laptop. I'll bring mine along."

Eric was a familiar figure at tournaments in Buffalo and other upper New York State events. Karen and he were on friendly terms. He arrived in short order and greeted Fred and Karen. They started right in on their discussion without introductions.

"One thing we have going for us is that we'll be looking at a very short time interval," said Fred. "Twelve-forty-five to one-fifteen, I'd say. Come to think of it, this might be interesting. A grand melee."

Eric asked, "Okay. Friday afternoon, early. That's what we're interested in?"

"That's the time. Have you got it?"

"I know the cameras were on. I'm not sure what we were recording at the time. I don't know what we'll find. I brought my own camera and laptop along. We'll be able to flip through the whole period. It's not that long anyway." Eric took out his cables, installed the flash drive in the camera and connected the camera to the laptop. He turned it on, fumbled for a while searching for the right spot to begin, then set it to play. "Here we are," he said. "This starts between twelve-thirty and twelve-forty-five. The action we're interested in took place in half an hour. I guess the evacuation took place right around one o'clock. We can just let it run and see if you spot anything interesting. It has a zoom function in case you want to look closer at some point."

They let the camera play the scenes it had captured. "I see you've focused on the playing area," said Fred.

"That's right," said Karen. "But let's keep looking. "We may see something that helps."

They watched the screen display repetitive, meaningless scenes of players shuffling around the room. The camera was sharp, and even with the variations in light in different parts of the ballroom, all of the people were clearly recognizable. They called out names of famous players as they passed by the lens of the camera. They all laughed when they saw two well-known characters having a spirited argument and gesturing vigorously.

"Love these silent movies," said Karen.

Karen got a start out of both of her colleagues when she whooped, "Whoa, right there."

Eric stopped the camera. "What's up?" he asked.

Karen's whoop had the effect of waking Clive. He emerged from his torpid state with a yell and continued his rhythmic solo for a few moments. Fred and Eric looked at each other and burst out laughing. "Sorry," said Karen. "Clive has very few social skills so far, but I'm working on them."

"Not to worry," said Fred. "He won't bother us."

Clive finally stopped his loud bawling and switched to random, meaningless babbling. Karen raised her voice so that she could be heard. "Someone just walked by who looked familiar. Can you put it in slow motion and stop it when I tell you?" she asked.

"Good as done." Eric did as requested, stopped when Karen asked, and zoomed in on the face Karen thought she had recognized.

"There," she said. "Doesn't that person resemble the composite we made up? Here. I've got a copy of Monday's Bulletin." She took a crumpled piece of newsprint out of her purse and smoothed out the wrinkles. The two directors looked at the picture on paper, then at the laptop screen, then back at the paper.

"I do see a resemblance," said Fred. "The person on TV is a man. He looks like a caddy. I think I've seen him around. He's not a familiar person, mind you."

Eric didn't recollect the person at all. "He's not wearing a caddy uniform. Let's zoom in a few more notches. Look. He's wearing a hotel uniform."

"So he is," said Karen. "Eric, can you possibly print off a still picture of this scene? Or put it this way, any scene where we have a good view of the person's face?"

"I can make a copy for you of the shot you're interested in. This will be a first for me, but my manual says I can do it. The quality of the image may not be good."

"Okay," said Karen. "At least we know that our person was on the scene at around the time the crime was committed. That confirms that one of our suspects was here and had the opportunity to carry out the crime. Please hang onto that film."

"It's actually a memory stick, not a film. Everything's digital. "

"I'll take what you can give me," said Karen.

"Give me an hour," said Eric. "I'll take this up to my room and work it a bit. I'll call you."

Marshall drew up his police car near a sign:

```
FRIENDLY PETS CLINIC
T. RUHE DVM
SMALL PETS WELCOME
```

Omaha's minimal rush hour traffic had not been an impediment, and they arrived after a short trip. There were a few cars in the parking lot.

"Looks like we're in business," said Lente.

"So far, so good," replied Marshall.

They entered the modern, attractive building and headed for the reception desk. A pretty girl in her early twenties greeted them cordially and asked if she could help.

"We're looking for Ted Ruhe," said Marshall. "Is he available?"

"I'm sorry, sir. There's no Ted Ruhe here. Dr. Ruhe's name is Tim, but everyone calls him Doctor. I don't know anyone named Ted Ruhe, but I can ask the doctor if he does."

"Could you do that, miss?" asked Marshall.

The young lady disappeared through a door which, when open, allowed barking and meowing sounds to reverberate through the reception area. The noises disappeared the instant the door shut. The sound effects repeated themselves as she returned with a large, fit, bald man in tow.

"This is Doctor Ruhe. Perhaps he can help you."

Tim Ruhe proved to be a genial middle-aged man who greeted them warmly. "Ted Ruhe is it? Yes, there is a Ted Ruhe in town who's a veterinarian. He doesn't have his own practice. I can give you his address. He works down in Lincoln. You know where that is?"

Marshall nodded affirmatively. "That's about an hour from here."

"Might be longer at this time of day. Ted works with cattle and large animals—you know, bison herds, elk, ostriches, that sort of thing. Darned good man, too. The ranchers all like him. I wouldn't touch that sort of work. Too dangerous. He got snapped on the ear by an angry ostrich a couple of years ago. Then he got a bad infection. Of course, bison are the worst. I prefer small animals."

Lente took out his carefully folded composite drawing of the suspect they were looking for. "Does your friend look like this?" he asked, holding the crumpled newsprint so that Ruhe had a good view.

Ruhe answered, "Yes. That's the man. He's better looking of course, but that's a decent likeness."

Marshall said, "We'd certainly appreciate information on where to find him."

Ruhe instructed his receptionist to look up the address and draw the men a map showing directions. "Can I ask what your business is?" he asked.

"I'm with the city police here," said Marshall, flashing identification. "My colleague is from Boston."

"Homicide," added Lente, with a note of pride.

"That so?" said Ruhe. "I don't suppose Ted's in any trouble."

"We're gathering facts right now. I'd appreciate it if you keep this under your hat."

"Of course. Always glad to help the police."

Marshall and Lente took the map offered by the receptionist and left. "We've just got to go about fifty miles southwest," said Marshall. "Won't take long."

Karen was delighted when Eric called and told her he had a couple of pictures ready. "I can bring them up if you like."

"That would be great. You're a dear."

Eric arrived a few minutes later. He and Karen laid out the two pictures he had printed off and compared them with the composite published in the Bulletin.

"A dead ringer," said Karen. "Look. He's got something slung over his shoulder, some kind of a bag. You can just see the strap and the top of the bag."

"That's right," agreed Eric.

"That would be the bag he used to carry his blowguns and darts in, and then lug away the money." She thanked Eric and he left.

When Art and Julia returned from their expedition to the suburbs, Karen was bubbling with enthusiasm. "Take a look at these," she said, and displayed her small photo gallery. "This is a blowup of a scene from the video cameras." She laid the two portraits Eric had produced beside the composite from the Bulletin. "How's that for a match?"

"Pretty good," said Art.

Karen continued, "These are from the room where the robbery took place. This person was standing around nearby. He was wearing a Westin uniform and had some kind of a bag slung over his shoulder."

Art added, "We have the Westin shirt. Found it at the place we just inspected. And we found out from the neighbor that we're almost certainly looking for a female. The people at the location have a niece named Barbara who visits occasionally."

Julia broke in. "I'd better call Bill Steele. He'll want to be dialed in at this point." The receptionist told her that Bill wasn't at his desk, so Julia identified herself and asked that Bill be interrupted in whatever he was doing and brought to the phone.

"Hi Julia. What's up?"

"I'm at the Westin downtown," she answered. "The whole case is heating up and I could use some help."

"Where are you exactly?" asked Bill.

"If you can make it, ask for Fraser's suite when you get here."

"I'll finish what I'm doing and get down as soon as I can," said Bill.

Julia hung up and turned her attention back to Art and Karen. "Bill Steele is going to join us. We can use him right now."

~  ~

Lente and Marshall arrived at a plain-looking, well-scrubbed complex with a sign out front identifying the business.

LINCOLN VETERINARIANS
LARGE ANIMALS OUR SPECIALTY
WE KNOW BULLS
OSTRICHES AND BISON WELCOME

"Looks like the place," said Lente.

They found the office building empty, and walked on to a large barn. They heard urgent bellowing interspersed with excited human voices coming from the inside. They hesitated briefly, wondering whether it was safe to enter. Lente peered in through a window. He could see a slight man wearing a rubber bathing hat and a yellow rain slicker who appeared to be directing traffic. He had two other, similarly clad people helping. One of them was holding some medical devices and the other was hosing down the floor with a stream of water. A chained bull was the center of attention, and seemed none too happy at being inspected. He didn't appreciate the hardware that restrained his movements, and was protesting loudly. The slight man noticed the officers at the door, and moved towards them. He smiled and came out of the barn to talk. He displayed the same Nebraskan geniality as the other Ruhe had. Lente was interested to note how closely the facial features of the man resembled the composite picture Karsh had provided.

"You gentlemen can't come in here, I'm sorry. I've got another hour's work with this bull. I can talk then if you want." This information was given in firm tones that were not at all offensive. "Why don't you wait in the office? You can help yourselves to a cup of coffee."

"We need to talk right away," said Marshall, displaying his police ID.

The man nodded to his colleagues and escorted the officers out into the yard. "You can see we're very busy right now. How can I help you?"

"Are you Doctor Ted Ruhe?"

"I sure am."

"You were in Boston recently?"

"I sure was."

"And you left in a hurry."

"I sure did."

"Can you tell us about it?" Lente continued.

"I got a call from the boss while I was there. He asked me if I could come right back. His biggest customer has a breeding business and he just put in an offer on some bulls. That can be an expensive proposition, as you might guess. A breeder can't afford to buy bad bulls, so we have to check them out before he pays for them. I'm the man that does all that—my specialty. I give them a complete physical, take a look at their reproductive system, measure the scrotum, take a semen sample and measure sperm count and motility. If you gentlemen would like to learn more, I can get you a set of clothes and you can join us. Of course, you'll have to sign a waiver."

The two officers had just learned more than they thought they would ever need to know about bulls. Lente fought hard to conceal his feeling of embarrassment.

"You're aware of the murder and robbery that took place in Boston while you were there?"

"Yes, I heard about that. I saw the Monday morning edition of the Bulletin. I think everybody did. They were all talking about it."

"Did you happen to notice the picture on the front page?" continued Lente.

"I took a quick look."

"Remind you of anyone?"

"As a matter of fact, it did. It looked a lot like my brother."

"Well, now," said Lente. "I suppose you and your brother look a lot alike."

"We do," said Ruhe. "But the face in the picture didn't have a big mole on the right cheek." Ruhe turned his face slightly so the officers could see a smooth, brown-colored mark, at least a square inch in size, showing prominently on the lower part of his right cheek.

"I see what you mean. You're aware that the murder weapon was a dart—the kind you fellows use to slow down animals?"

"No. I wasn't aware of that."

"The darts were delivered by a blowgun. We understand you've bought plenty of these devices."

"I sure have. We use them all the time. You can't beat them if you want to slow down an ostrich. Is that strange?"

"Not strange at all unless they're used as a murder weapon."

"I couldn't agree more. You think someone used a blowgun as a murder weapon?"

"That's what killed our victim. The person responsible for this murder knew a lot about darts and blowguns. We'd like to know about your activities in Boston last Friday."

"Last Friday? That's no problem. I was visiting a colleague at Tufts University. They have a big veterinarian school in Grafton. That's about forty miles from downtown. They run a large animal hospital for horses, cattle, even llamas. I like to keep up to date in my field."

"Can you give us the name of someone you were with during the day? What about lunch time?"

"Certainly. I had lunch out in Grafton with an old friend I went to school with. I can give you all the details. Look, I've got to get back to my bull. I can't leave him like this in the middle of an inspection."

Marshall felt it was time to step in. "Thanks for your cooperation, Dr. Ruhe. We'll let you get back to your work. Get us the information on your friend." He handed Ruhe a card with contact information. "We'll be in touch to check out the details." Marshall was thinking that the odds of their returning were about as likely as he and Lente becoming matadors. They shook hands with Ruhe and left.

Marshall said, "Well, that clears the mud out of that. Let's head back to town and have lunch. Sebastian's is making my mouth water. I can just see a little twenty-ounce porterhouse sitting there on my plate."

"Step on it," said Lente.

Firm banging on the door of the hotel suite interrupted the conversation. Art showed Bill Steele into the suite. "Glad you're able to join us, Bill," said Art. "We're starting to make some progress now."

Bill said, "That's good to hear. I'd appreciate a full review to bring me up to speed. Then we can figure how to help each other."

Art traced the thread of evidence that had led Julia and him to investigate a home in a Boston suburb. Bill said, "I hadn't heard about the place you're talking about."

Art responded, "The Grahams' place. We talked to a neighbor and got a key to look around. The neighbor says that a niece lived there for a while and then moved away, but visited off and on. That confirms that we're looking for a female. Our suspect stayed there for who knows how long and left an item of clothing behind that positively confirmed her presence. It was a shirt with a Westin logo on it."

Karen passed around the pictures that Eric Bolls had printed off from the video surveillance. She explained the setup to Bill, and showed that, alongside the composite picture in the Bulletin, they had almost a perfect match.

Julia said, "I've run the composite picture through our Boston database and got zero. I sent it off to the FBI yesterday."

Karen said, "The other thought I had, and it's more of a nagging feeling than a logical thought, is why has no one outside of the bridge group spotted this person? She had to have been around the hotel for three or four days. No one noticed her?"

Art added, "She did a pretty good job of disguising her looks. Papan and Jose, the hotel employees who saw the perp in the washrooms just before the robbery, both mentioned that they thought they saw a man. But what they really saw was a thin person of a certain age. Anyone could cut her hair, put on some unflattering clothes, and parade around like a man. Picture someone thin with very little figure. Dyeing hair, wearing a wig, all those steps can change an identity easily. And a gender. What better way to hide your presence than to have a big search on for a man when you dress up as a woman?"

Steele asked, "Did Karsh get into different colors of hair in his work?"

Art replied, "He did. But hair is the least permanent feature of a suspect. It's the easiest feature to change. Anyway, that's history. We have a huge incentive to resolve the case by the end of the week. When the tournament finishes on Sunday night, everyone will either be leaving or thinking about it. By noon Monday, there won't be a soul left. All of the actors, witnesses, suspects, anybody who can really help us, will have disappeared."

"We'll need a big break to polish it off by then," replied Bill. "Could happen. With three of us on the case, our odds are better."

"Four," said Art. "Don't forget Karen."

"My apologies," said Bill, nodding and smiling at Karen.

Karen added, "Five, if you count Clive."

Art said, "We know the murder weapon, or at least what it looks like. We have a photograph now, and that's always a notch better than a composite drawing."

Bill said, "It's quite possible that she's been operating right under your noses all along, and nobody spotted her. How do we locate her? We can't search a thousand rooms without an army. Did you show all of the hotel staff the picture Karsh produced for us?"

"I showed it to everyone I could. We posted it down in the lobby where the receptionists work. And the concierge desk. Those people see everyone coming and going. I gave a copy to Chris and he posted it on the Bulletin board where his employees get their assignments and other info. Did we show all of the hotel staff? No. But we did cover most of them."

Bill persisted with his questions. "And the hotel employees gave you nothing? Maybe I ought to spend some time with the hotel staff. Sometimes a second round of questions gets different answers."

"An official badge can sometimes make a big impression," said Art.

Julia broke in. "Say, guys. You know the neighbor, Grace Mayores, that Art and I met?"

"Sure," said Art.

"She could get us a phone number for the owners of the place—the Grahams. They must know a lot about our friend Bobby Rideau. She said the niece's name was Barbara."

"Good idea. I think we're ready for that."

Julia went ahead with her call, made a note in the middle of the call and turned to the group. "I have a number for the Grahams," she reported.

"Great," said Art. "We'd better get hold of them right away. How about if I call them and you two listen in. I can introduce you or leave you out, as you wish. Probably best to leave you out. The Grahams are an old couple and they may be more at ease talking to one person."

When Art dialed the Florida number, a woman picked up on the second ring. "Ann speaking." Although a slight tremble in her voice betrayed her as elderly, she proved to be anything but reticent. When Art finished introducing himself, she said, "Now why don't you introduce the other folks with you? I can hear them breathing."

The Boston trio burst out laughing. "Touché," said Art, who introduced his companions and outlined the reason for their call. "The person we're looking for uses the name Bobby Rideau. Or perhaps Bobby Rainbow. Do those names mean anything to you?"

Ann called her husband to an extension, and then said, "Bobby Rideau? Rainbow? I'm not sure. We have a niece named Barbara Rindle. Is that possible?"

"Anything is possible at this point," said Art. "The person we're looking for used your house recently."

"That could be Barbara. We gave her a key and told her to come and go as she wants. We hardly see her."

"Sounds like you're very trusting," said Art.

"We took her in when she was thirteen," said Ann. "She ran away from her own home. My sister never sent for her or came to get her. We gave her a roof over her head and did what we could for her. That was about all. She was so headstrong. John and I had no children and we were financially sound. We let Barbara come and go as she pleased. We couldn't teach her any values. No ethics, no religion. You have to understand that she had a terrible childhood. My sister and her husband gave her a dreadful home. No home at all. Her whole childhood was one downward spiral after another. When she was six, a mortgage company took over the family home. Then her parents' marriage broke up."

Her husband spoke up. "She was a healthy girl, always trim. Unfortunately, she was always a grim person. She hardly ever smiled. She was always far too serious to attract a man."

"Where does she normally live?" asked Art. "Not with you, I presume."

Ann answered, "She moves around a lot. Her last address was in Portland, Oregon. I can get it for you."

She returned to the phone and gave Art a number. Art thanked the Grahams and hung up. "The name Barbara Rindle rings a bell." He looked at Karen.

"That name is on our list from Ughdart. And there's a bridge pro by that name, isn't there?" she asked.

Art replied, "I think so. You know who could tell us? John Sabin. He knows every pro on the circuit plus all the scoop we'd ever want. Why don't we get him in here? He's sure to be playing somewhere. I'll go down and get hold of Fred Jardeen. Fred will track him down."

Art collected the empty cups and took them to the sink.

"Someone's trained him." Bill smiled at Karen.

"You used the past tense," she replied. "It's an ongoing program."

Sabin was easy to find. He was playing in a knockout event, dressed in his customary jacket-and-tie uniform. An elderly man with gray hair and a slightly stooped posture, he was known universally throughout the world of competitive bridge. Although he never competed in national events, he came to the national tournaments regularly because his customers liked the crowds and the big masterpoint awards that were available. Gracious as always, he apologized for having to close out the session with his customer, but agreed to come to Art's suite as soon as the game finished.

When he arrived in the presidential suite, Art introduced him to the detectives and explained that they wanted information on Barbara Rindle.

John spoke with a Carolina drawl that was easy to listen to. "I know Barbara Rindle pretty well. I suppose she's in trouble again. Can't seem to avoid it. A couple of years ago, I had a special relationship with her. Not the kind you think. She's chronically unemployed. She did some work as a caddy, just working local tournaments, sectional and regional events. She'd never come to a national tournament. I got to know her when she was a caddy. We got to be real good friends. You know, I believe that if I want to be a good pro, I make friends with everyone. It can't hurt. She started to play bridge a bit while she was a caddy, and she had a good mind for it. Real good mind. She used to come over and ask me endless questions. I never took any money from her. But I never turned her down any time she wanted to ask something. I was happy to loan her all my books. Old books, new books, magazines, hard covers, everything I had. I have quite a collection, too. She ate them all up. Returned most of them, too.

She got to be good, real good, fast. She found she had genuine talent for the game. It didn't take long for her serious study to pay off and she developed into a pretty good player. She started a winning streak. Either she'd win an event or she'd place in the top ten regularly. I told her she ought to become a professional player. I thought she had nothing to lose by trying it out for a while. Of course, she had no money to live on. I told her I'd lend her a few bucks. She could pay me back when she started getting customers. Hotel rooms mostly have two beds for the same price. I'm not rich, but I get mine paid for by my customers, and as long as I had a room, she was welcome to share."

"So she decided to quit caddying. She dressed herself up and tried being a pro. It took a while. I told her she had to quit being so gosh-danged serious. She never impressed any of the men who hired pros. I don't recall her ever having a male client. But she developed a knack for getting on well with female clients. She was able to establish a decent reputation and connected with enough wealthy ladies who were willing to pay her to play with them. She built up a decent practice as a pro.

"I said I knew her because she was a professional bridge player, but not anymore. She had this flock of clients who were happy to pay her a modest fee. She was like me, in a way. I never made it to the top tier of pros and never will. We give the customers lessons after every session, or in groups when they prefer. We get steady work, but we don't have much money left over after expenses.

"Results come in cycles. We hit good streaks when all our decisions seem to click. We all hit periods when luck turns. Worse luck follows bad luck. With me, I always came out of it. I don't spend much. I can always go fishing if I get fed up. In her case, her reputation started to slip along with her income. She thought she might try something 'a little extra' to improve masterpoint production. Unfortunately, she did this at a time when the ACBL had introduced video cameras into the playing areas of their games, and swung them around at random until they captured something interesting. Something interesting occurred when Barbara, in a Swiss team event, with no one else at her table, dealt a couple of hands with several cards face up, and then put the cards in the boards. I guess she got away with it and started to think she could do it regularly. Then the folks manning the camera thought they saw something on one of the videos. Once you've been suspected of cheating, they give you lots of show time. They caught her a few times, not just once, and when they called Barbara in to view the videos, she had no choice but to disappear from the scene. They left her crying when they forced her to resign from the ACBL. I haven't seen her since that time. I know that her income was cut off, and her lifestyle totally exploded."

Julia asked, "Did you see the picture we posted on the Bulletin a few days ago?"

"Monday?" said John. "Yes, I did. I guess what confused me was that the picture was definitely a male. I didn't give it a second thought. Now that you mention it, I missed the whole point."

"Wow," said Karen.

Art spoke. "We have Rindle's Portland address. Probably that's where she is now. You might check the local banking system to trace an account associated with her. I bet we'll have prints on the bridge bucks or the bag we found in the room. Either of those ought to get your D.A. onside."

"Maybe she's on a plane to Portland right now," said Bill. "Either that or she'll be there by now. We could put a trace on the airlines and see if her credit card was used in the past few days. Julia, you have the credit card number. Why don't we make a couple of calls?"

"Here we go."

While Julia got the credit card information, Art fired up his laptop and looked up flights from Boston to Portland. He printed off details of afternoon flights from seven airlines. Julia phoned the airlines and gave each the same request—to phone her if a flight had been booked using the credit card number she read out.

Within half an hour, US Air returned her call. "We have a Barbara Rindle using the credit card number you provided. She left on Monday on our three p.m. flight to Portland. It connected in Chicago and arrived in Portland at eight oh three."

"Just what we wanted," said Julia. "Thanks very much." She relayed the information to her colleagues.

Bill said, "Now, we've got to contact the Portland police force and get someone to track her down. I know a guy in Portland homicide who'll help us."

"Charlie Kingston?" asked Art.

"You know him?"

"I worked with him on a case a few years ago."

"I guess everyone knows Charlie. Do we think our suspect is dangerous?" asked Steele.

"She's a menace," said Karen. "A robber and a killer."

"You won't have a problem isolating her and transferring her back here," said Art.

Julia piped up, "We need to involve Bert Orchnay at the D.A.'s office. There's some required paper work if we want the Portland group to help us."

"You're right," admitted Bill. "I'll talk to Bert right now."

"There is a point to think about. I suppose one or both of you will go to Portland and help with the arrest?" queried Art.

"Probably both," said Bill. "And to bring her back."

"Okay. You may get into plea-bargaining. That's between you, your D.A. and the suspect. You might consider whether any or all of the remaining money can be retrieved. I'm sure the league would be charmed if they got some of their entry fees back."

"That shouldn't be a problem," answered Bill. "No promises, but I'm sure the issue will come up. Her lawyer will want the charges reduced to manslaughter. That's obvious. I suppose he could ask for leniency in case she makes a full confession. We'll see how it goes and work it in as best we can."

"Great," said Art. "We'll be heading back tomorrow, unless Alan wants us longer. I imagine we've done enough damage to his budget already. I'll give you our Florida number."

Bill asked, "Julia, should we get in touch with Bruce and let him know the status of the case?"

Julia laughed, "Right now, I expect he's heading back from Omaha with a Doctor Ruhe in handcuffs."

CHAPTER 9

A FLAMING REDHEAD WITH BRIGHT LIPSTICK approached the registration desk at the Westin. She fidgeted noticeably as she waited her turn, then announced her name as Bobby Rainbow. She mentioned that her account was all prepaid, and said she was checking out. The clerk observed that her customer appeared as nervous as a starving cat, but she had been trained to deal with many personality types, after all. The transaction was completed quickly, and the clerk wished the customer a good day and thought nothing more about the incident.

The redhead shivered momentarily as she stepped outside the hotel. She was happy to feel the warmth inside the cab that took her from the Westin hotel to Logan Airport. Her words of approval to the driver were the most polite she had spoken all day. As they traveled, the driver discovered quickly that his efforts at small talk were going to be about as productive as a conversation with Boston pigeons. When they arrived at the US Air terminal, she paid her fare, grabbed her bag and disappeared from the taxi driver's sight into the milling crowd. After spotting the check-in kiosk, the redhead hurried over and picked up her one-way ticket to Portland. Next stop was the airport bar where she calmed her nerves by gulping two shots of Barton's gin on the rocks. After six hours of uneventful flying, she got off the plane and took a taxi home.

Home was her bare-bones condominium. Barbara Rindle was the outright owner of the property thanks to the generosity of Ann Graham and her husband. The basic necessities like heating, air-conditioning and running water all worked fine and were included in condo fees. The colors were drab and unimaginative. The furnishings were plain, sturdy, and all second-hand. It wasn't much, but it was her cave—a safe haven that she could always come back to. She loved it. The neighborhood was poor, and, although the people were friendly, no one ever bothered her here. One snarl was usually enough to discourage neighbors from pursuing intimacy or friendship. Her problem had always been that she could barely afford the monthly fees. *That's about to change,* she thought.

When her family home broke up, Barbara's mother had sent her to spend time with her aunt and uncle. What started out as a brief visit became a long-term situation. It was the only lasting, good event that happened in her life. They had no reason to help her, except for their own instinctive humanity.

Comfortable financially, with no children of their own, they made Barbara feel welcome and encouraged her to stay as long as she chose. They did everything they could for her, including buying the condo unit and making her the owner.

Her parents' breakup was a final straw in a series of hateful events. She couldn't understand it and could never forgive them. Getting out from under the torment of her mother's presence was a huge stroke of luck for Barbara, but by then nothing could have changed her behavior. School was a bore. Although life on Thorncrest Avenue with the Grahams left her with no material wants, she could never pull herself out of a deep, cynical view of life. After barely passing high school, a friend convinced her that living in the West would be a neat idea. The Grahams made no attempt to stop her and even encouraged her to find employment and settle down at work she might like.

She liked Portland, especially the winters, and was able to bring in a little money with part-time work at fast-food outlets. She never worked at one place long enough to get past a minimum wage. One of her friends told her about a caddying job at bridge tournaments. She tried it at small tournaments in nearby locations, but never found enough work to earn more than pocket change. She did find, however, that her razor-sharp mind was admirably adapted to the game. Occasional play led to frequent games and then to a deep addiction. Trumps, notrump, bidding conventions, squeezes, endplays—the whole gamut of the finer points of the game totally fascinated her. A veteran bridge professional named John Sabin became a friend and a mentor to her, and helped her develop into a skilled player. Eventually, he encouraged her to try her hand at being a bridge professional. After a good start, Barbara's lack of common sense converted decent career prospects into a humiliating disaster. She was caught cheating and ejected from the league, banned from playing anywhere in league competitions. She developed a deep hatred for the bridge league.

It was hard to like Barbara. With a lifelong habit of rudeness, she came across as being as friendly as a snapping turtle. Her manner of speaking to everyone was impulsive and callous. This was so off-putting that deeply buried virtues seldom showed through. Few of her acquaintances got to appreciate her high intelligence, her speed with numbers, or her very quick wit. She often felt guilty about the way she spoke, especially to her aunt and uncle. They always came up smiling after one of her blasts, and she wrote this off as a sign of meekness or lack of understanding of the problems of a young person.

After her disastrous bridge experience, she returned to her condo in Portland and undertook another series of part-time jobs. She heard about an internship program at the Portland zoo, where a few months of part-time volunteer work under the direction of a professional could lead to a permanent position as a technician. She had always liked animals and decided to look into the opportunity. She was happy to be accepted into the program and found the work to her liking.

One of the veterinarians invited her to help with the vaccination of a newly born pair of bobcat twins. The vet explained how he used his blowgun, loaded the darts with immobilizing chemicals, installed the darts one at a time, and launched them at his target. On the day of their vaccination task, the vet approached the mother cat from the outside of the bars, launched his missile, and said, "Look, Barbara. It takes only seconds to put them to sleep. I'd like you to pick up each kitten and hold it for me so I can vaccinate and record them. We have to be out of here before the mother comes to or we'll have a ruckus on our hands. Let's work quickly now."

They entered the cage and Barbara picked up the beautiful kittens one by one and held them for the vet. She noticed their still-closed eyes, their soft, spotted fur, tiny paws without claws and mouths without teeth. They had not yet developed their mother's vicious mannerisms; they were still gentle. Barbara and the vet finished their work in good time and left the cage just as the mother was shaking off the effects of the drug. The experience fascinated Barbara and she became expert at immobilizing small animals using darts.

Unfortunately, once she completed her internship, Barbara's lack of social skills could not get her out of the bottom position on the shortlist of applicants. The only work she was offered was a seasonal, part-time job in either security or food service. Barbara did what she had to—she took advantage of work as a security guard for a few months and faced up to the issue of planning where her future meals would come from.

With plenty of time to dream, she began to fantasize about how wonderful it would be to get her hands on a decent sum of money. She thought of a nice car, upgrading her condominium, and plenty of other items that she had never been able to afford. She hit upon the idea of relieving the bridge league of a sizable sum of money. The more she thought about it, the more she liked the notion. It would achieve two goals: provide a good sum of money and gain revenge against people who had done her wrong. After running several schemes through her head, she came up with a detailed plan that she felt could be successful.

The days leading up to the robbery had been an emotional roller coaster. Four or five times, she had been on the brink of calling the whole scheme off.

Jail, disgrace, letting down her aunt and uncle in Boston, all of these possibilities had weighed on her mind. Another week at her job pounding around the zoo as a security official, examining and tagging cars parked in improper places, looking for intruders who never appeared, checking cage gates that were never unlocked, all for what seemed like the zillionth time, cemented her decision. *To hell with it*, she thought. *I'm not doing this for a lifetime. There's nothing else I'm good for. Nobody wants me. If I don't get out and get some money myself, nobody will do it for me.* She finally made up her mind to go ahead with the scheme.

~  ~

After a long cab ride from the Portland airport, she entered her condo, breathed a long sigh of relief and went to her bedroom. She tossed her bag and red wig on the bed, hung her coat in the closet, and took the remains of her stolen money from her bag. She had the perfect place to hide it. A small trap door opened to an attic area over her closet. She could easily reach in by standing on a chair and moving the trap door out of the way. This had all been part of her plan. She laid the money on her bed and counted out a bit over nineteen thousand dollars. A thrill sent shivers up and down her spine. All hers! When she had the money safely stowed away in a cardboard box, she closed the trap door, lay down on her bed, shut her eyes and relaxed.

By the end of her second day at home, Barbara's feelings were starting to stabilize. She was on top of the world. A blessed feeling that she was safe began to set in. She had pulled it off! Now that she had the money securely hidden in her condo, she felt sure that no one would ever find it. Maybe she had finally completed a successful project.

Shortly before noon on the Friday following her arrival home, her doorbell rang. Her heart pounded. She was not expecting anyone. A glance out of her living room window revealed an unfamiliar, unmarked car on the street. She couldn't see who was ringing. She went to the door and was confronted by a group of two men and a woman. Charley Kingston was in his home territory and it fell to him to take the lead.

"Barbara Rindle?" he asked.

"Yes."

"We need to question you on a robbery and murder in Boston."

"What in hell are you talking about?" Barbara's voice was somewhere between a squeak and a scream.

Kingston showed his identification, along with a warrant to take Barbara to Portland Police headquarters for questioning. He introduced Julia and Bill from Boston. "We'll all have fewer problems if you come quietly," he said.

"You bastards," responded Barbara. She thought about making a break, or refusing to cooperate. Three-to-one odds made any action on her part absolute foolishness. She decided to bide her time and go along with the group. "Let me get my coat."

"I'll come with you," offered Julia.

This produced a scowl from Barbara, but there was little she could do to stop the cop. Julia followed her to the hall, cautious as a cat, ready for almost anything that Barbara might decide to do, but the trip to the closet was short and without incident. Barbara was silent and cooperative during the drive to the Portland police station. The police officers had agreed that structured questioning in the atmosphere of the station, where everything could be taped, was preferable to blurting out questions and answers in a moving car.

The ride had the effect of building more tension inside Barbara. She was ready to burst when she entered the station and took a seat. Kingston introduced a public defender who would assist Barbara at no cost to her, and the lawyer informed her of her rights. Julia reviewed the main events of the crime aloud for all the hear—purchases of blowguns, darts, and chemicals; the robbery; the room traced to Barbara; the discovery of the currency used by the league. When she came to the death of Hank, Barbara's brave front collapsed.

She shouted, "I didn't mean to kill him. I don't know what happened." She broke down and began to sob convulsively.

"If the remaining money is returned, we will be as lenient as the law allows," said Kingston.

"How about it, Barbara?" asked the public defender, gently.

Barbara tearfully nodded agreement, then went into a shell and offered no further communication.

Julia and Bill exchanged a long look over the head of their prisoner. At Bill's stern nod of approval, Julia stood fractionally taller and a spark was in her eye as she took Barbara by the elbow, urged her to her feet, and steered her out the door.

CHAPTER 10

ART BOOKED A FLIGHT TO DAYTONA BEACH for three in the afternoon and then announced to Karen that they would have to leave shortly after one, but that prior to that, they would be having a big lunch to celebrate. Two room-service stewards arrived at eleven-thirty, each with a good-sized trolley in tow. With appropriate flourishes, they set up the large dining room table with a white linen tablecloth and napkins. After placing half a dozen red roses in the center, they gestured to the Frasers to sit down.

Art said, "I assume you're not still on the wagon."

"Unfortunately I am. And actually, I don't miss it at all."

"So I'll have to drink a whole bottle of CAVA myself?"

"Well—" said Karen. "I guess a little bit—"

"Won't hurt," finished Art. He signaled to a steward to serve two glasses of bubbly.

The stewards next brought out two silver platters, each with a dozen oysters. Mercifully, Clive seemed interested in the activities of the stewards and remained silent.

Art proposed a toast, and added, "Here's to a long list of successful cases."

"Yes, indeed. You'll need them to pay for this," said Karen, sipping happily and munching oysters.

"Don't throw cold water on my little party," responded Art. "Anyway, I met with Alan Gilead this morning. He was all smiles."

"That'll pay a lot of bills."

"Don't worry. This is going on my expense account. He knows we wrapped this up much faster than anyone could have believed. We also ended up way under budget. Even after adding the lunch."

"Your price was too low."

"He says they expect to recover a good part of the money that Rindle got away with. That'll cover my fee several times over. While he was in a good mood, I asked him if I could put one more lunch on the bill. I didn't specify what the lunch was going to be, just that I'd put it on the room bill. He said to go ahead."

The stewards cleared away the oyster shells, refilled champagne glasses and served lobster rolls. The final touch was a small helping of crème caramel, which Art knew to be Karen's favorite dessert. "Oooh," said Karen appreciatively.

Over coffee, she asked, "Well, you've had your first taste of life as a private detective. How did it feel?"

"Terrible. Low pay and no perks at all."

"Back to Buffalo?"

"Not a chance."